dermaphoria

A NOVEL BY CRAIG CLEVENGER

dermaphoria

A NOVEL BY CRAIG CLEVENGER

Lawson Library
A Division of MacAdam/Cage Publishing
155 Sansome Street, Suite 550
San Francisco, CA 94104
www.macadamcage.com

Excerpts from the work of Geoffrey Sonnabend are courtesy of the Museum of Jurassic Technology.
Where the Wild Roses Grow, copyright Nick Cave. Used with permission from Mute Song, Ltd.

Library of Congress Cataloging-in-Publication Data
Clevenger, Craig, 1964-
  Dermaphoria / by Craig Clevenger.
    p. cm.
  ISBN 1-931561-75-3 (alk. paper)
  1. Los Angeles (Calif.)–Fiction. 2. Loss (Psychology)–Fiction.
3. Criminals–Fiction. 4. Memory–Fiction. I. Title.
  PS3603.L49D47 2005
  813'.6–dc22

                                                                    2005020095

Paperback edition: September 2006
ISBN-10: 1-59692-102-1
ISBN-13: 978-1-59692-102-1

Manufactured in the United States of America
10 9 8 7 6 5 4 3 2 1

Book and jacket design by Dorothy Carico Smith.

Publisher's Note: This is a work of fiction. Names, characters, places, and incidents either are the product of the author's imagination or are used fictitiously. Any resemblance to actual events, locales, or persons, living or dead, is entirely coincidental.

To Jill Nani

We, amnesiacs all, condemned to live in an eternally
fleeting present, have created the most elaborate of human
constructions, memory, to buffer ourselves against the
intolerable knowledge of the irreversible passage of time
and irretrievability of its moments and events.

—GEOFFREY SONNABEND

Obliscence: Theories of Forgetting and the Problem of Matter

From the first day I saw her I knew that she was the one
As she stared in my eyes and smiled
For her lips were the colour of the roses
That grew down the river, all bloody and wild

—NICK CAVE

"Where the Wild Roses Grow," *Murder Ballads*

I PANICKED AND SWALLOWED A HANDFUL OF FIREFLIES AND BLACK WIDOWS the inferno had not. Shiny glass teardrops shattered between my teeth while the fireflies popped like Christmas bulbs until I coughed up blood and blue sparks, starting another fire three inches behind my eyes and burning a hole through the floor of my memory. A lifetime of days, years, minutes and months, gone, but for a lone scrap, scorched and snagged on a frayed nerve ending and snapping in the breeze:

Desiree.

Hard as I try, a given recollection's pictures, sounds and smells, synchronized and ordered first to last, are everything but, swarming back through the cold hole in my brain where they hit the waning light and crackle into smoke. Others wait until dark to show themselves. I can hold a picture's fragments together for a lucid half second before a light shines through my eyes and they scatter, slipping between my brain's blackened cracks. One memory after the next turns yellow at the edges and crumbles to flakes at my touch.

I smell rotted pulp, old newspapers crawling with silverfish, the dank, dissolving bindings of books I don't remember reading. The stench gives me chills that turn to sandpaper on my neck and shoulders. My back burns if I lean the wrong way and I feel bandages but I can't touch them. My wrists and feet are cuffed to a chair in a room built to the stark schematics of my own head. Peeling walls the color of fingernails, cement floor, an overhead light with an orbiting moth. I'm alone with three machines. Two are on pause behind me, a third speaks into a telephone near the door.

"I miss you, Snowflake…I love you too…bunches…bunches and bunches…yes, Mommy too," his baritone whisper like the rumble of a distant train.

The machines are good. Whoever made them has all of my respect. Stunning detail in their faces, each loaded with a databank of behaviors for random interval display, all manner of mannerisms from coughs to sniffs, synthetic-cartilage knuckle cracks, biting lips and picking nails. The odor of static, the electric smell from a bank of new television sets gives them away.

"When I get home…okay, I will. Love you…bye bye, Snowflake." Faint dial tone, the ping ping of the doomed but determined moth against the lightbulb, then the machine sits in front of me.

"My daughter's been sick and I've been on overtime." He speaks to me as though I'm a sleeping child and he's about to kiss my forehead. He slides a cigarette from a pack with gold foil and some French name I can't pronounce.

"Haven't seen her for three days." The snap of his chrome lighter chimes like a coin hitting the pavement. "You smoke?"

He's engineered for sincerity and affection. The two behind me hide their eyes behind dark glasses, but his are exposed and big, liquid brown, radiating trust along with his voice. He wears an oiled-back, matinee-idol haircut and a tailored suit the deep blue of beetle wings and from across the table my eyes can feel the fabric, soft as a baby bird's throat. He's wired to smell like breath mints, cigarettes and expensive aftershave.

A tentacle of smoke gathers into a cloud overhead. It dissolves in the air between us and the smell stings my nose.

"No." Conscious of my manners with him, I correct myself. "No.

Thanks."

"I wasn't offering. Word is you can't remember to chew before you swallow. I'm just seeing for myself. How 'bout it? You remember smoking? Maybe falling asleep after a few drags?"

Shaking my head hurts, pulls at my skin.

"You did it on purpose. Covering your tracks?"

His circuits pause midbreath. The smoke above freezes into a ball of cobwebs. The moth is eavesdropping and I can hear the blood moving through my ears.

"You have any idea why you're talking to me?"

"Pieces of an idea." My blood beats louder and I think I'm going to be sick, "Who are you?"

"My name is Detective Nicholas Anslinger."

The slack in my chains is barely enough for me to reach his outstretched hand, sheathed in a synthetic polymer, mimicking my own skin.

"You can call me Detective," he continues. "Tell me these pieces."

I remember fire, but not starting one.

"I can't remember," he says. "I've heard this before." His brown eyes don't blink. They stay locked onto me. The damp draft unfurls a ribbon of cigarette smoke and coils it around my face.

"Let's start with the spiders. How many have you made and how many are still out there?"

Which is stranger, that Anslinger thinks I'm God or that he can chain God to a wheelchair beneath a spotlight?

"Try this," he says, leaning forward, "we found the galaxy."

He's right, I am God. It's all coming back to me. Darkness and light, floods, seven days and angels feuding amongst themselves for my favor. I lost my temper and the firestorm killed my precious dinosaurs. Work it out, learn to compromise, I told them. After the platypus, I disbanded the committee and stayed solo. This created resentment, a permanent rift in the organization.

Anslinger reads from a notebook, "1964 Ford, two-door, hardtop, candy apple red Galaxie 500, registered to one Eric Ashworth. Fully restored, if you don't count the blown back windshield and scorched paint." He snaps the notebook shut. "Nice ride."

I'm not God. I'm Eric Ashworth. It's all coming back to me.

No, it's not.

My head goes dark so the bugs will come crawling out. I squint through the blackness. I remember the sound of God cracking open the sky and shaking the earth. A ball of fire rising from a flaming house. Nails melting like slivers of silver wax. Beams and shingles collapsing into a pile of burning dust and the earth spitting them into the air. The angry fire boulder rolls down from the sky toward me. I run, choking back the spiders and fireflies fighting their way up my throat. More bugs will drop from the air at any second. Armored insects with polished, carbon fiber heads, giant eyes that shine like black mercury and can see in the dark.

A phone booth surrounded by nothing, and beyond the nothing, darkness. An invisible swarm burrows into my back, chewing through my skin as I call for help from the phone in the middle of nowhere. A light hits me from behind. I turn, face to face with a six-foot storm trooper mantis covered in armor plating, locked onto me with black goggle eyes. I crush it with the heavy plastic receiver before it eats my head and learns everything I know.

As little sense as this makes to Anslinger, it makes less to me.

"Your car was the only vehicle parked outside that house, of which there is nothing left. You assaulted the state trooper who found you at an abandoned gas station talking into a dead telephone. You were about an hour on foot from the burn site. The middle of the night, you could have died of exposure."

"I killed a bug." The bandages burn, my mind's eye sees a stretch of oily black blisters and the healthy skin peeling back like the paint on these walls.

Pieces come together. Okay, I've got it. They crumble apart. I move my thumb, then try to remember moving my thumb. Got it again. Play each preceding second one by one. Whole minutes, chunks of hours follow suit, binding to the fresh fragile moment before until the sequence holds.

My feet and wrists strapped to a bed frame surrounded by bags, tubes and beeping boxes. A machine dressed in white lets me suck on ice chips and says I'm going to be okay. They cut skin from my legs and sewed it onto my back, he says. Another machine in white asks me questions and shows me photographs so I can make up stories for them. I draw pictures, work puzzles and piss into cups. The machine gives me a notebook. Writing things down will help my memory. The first machine slides a syringe into one of the tubes. I follow the surge of liquid down to the crook of my elbow but nothing's there but a wad of cotton held with tape, my hands cuffed below a metal table and Anslinger sitting across from me.

My brain tries to kick-fire itself into working again. Nanostorm lightning burns the memory nest to a cinder, the drones thrown to their backs, legs kicking the air.

"This is the part where we sweat you, tag team good cop, bad cop," Anslinger says. "Those are the rules, right? Not my style. You're not in good shape. You rest for a while and we'll talk again."

Anslinger grinds out his cigarette.

"I've been looking for you, or someone like you, for some time. Beginning to think you were an urban legend. Don't take this the wrong way, but it's good to finally meet you."

two

BLEACHED WHITE SURROUNDS ME, VOID OF SHADOWS. THE WALLS COULD BE three feet from my fingers or thirty. My first instinct says I'm in Hell. My second instinct says the Devil doesn't like me and my third says he can afford a better suit. He's talking rapid-fire, like he's been ranting at me while I've been in a coma.

"You will talk to no one about your case without me. Period. Not the cops, not Anslinger, nobody. If any doctors ask you anything not pertaining to your treatment, you keep your mouth shut. Same for any orderlies or nurses. Especially for them. You don't talk to anyone while you're in here, and when you're out, you do likewise. Anyone with whom you speak can be subpoenaed, or worse, they could be a snitch or even undercover. Am I clear? Am I getting through to you?"

He speaks without stopping for breath or my answer.

"You say you can't remember anything so, if and when you start, the prosecution will accuse you of selective recall and slowly gut you in front of the jury. Did you know they tried to get you to waive your right to counsel?"

"No." I'm trying to hold his words together but they're piling up too quickly, old seconds crushed beneath the weight of the new.

"Yes, they did. But you couldn't sign your own name, let alone remember it. Things could have been worse. So remember, you talk to nobody about your case. Tell me you'll remember."

"I will."

"Say it."

"I'll remember."

"Remember what?"

"I won't talk to anyone about my case without you."

My case. I have a case. I've run a red light or I've been caught with a severed head in a paper bag. I'm scared to ask.

"We pleaded no contest. The judge set your bail at $50,000 for assaulting that state trooper and I've got a bondsman taking care of it. He owes me a favor, otherwise you'd be stuck here because you've got no credit or collateral. You'll be released by this afternoon."

"So, I've already been in court."

"You spent your arraignment in a wheelchair, drooling with your eyes open."

"And you and I have met."

"Yes." He clenches his jaw like he's about to hit me.

"You and I met, and I told you to keep your mouth shut, and then you promptly forgot. Heard you had a visit with Detective Anslinger."

"Anslinger, yeah. I thought the cops were robots." More sound of rushing blood. "He's a good guy," I add. "I like him."

"Stop liking him. And stop interrupting me. Okay, the bad news. The DA is going to try to convince a grand jury that you were the one making the stuff you OD'd on. Some combination of methamphetamine and LSD. The hospital says it nearly killed you and your long-term health is a crapshoot. Your heart stopped and they clocked you dead for eight seconds. You know what a firefly is?"

"It's a bug that glows in the dark. They shock you when you bite them open."

"Wrong. I mean the acid that's been turning up all over Los Angeles and creeping up the coast and inland for the last year. They think it's yours."

His last sentence hangs in the air between us. I'm supposed to grab for it, but I can't. He rolls his eyes and continues.

"They've connected you to the lab that blew, and Anslinger's crew has walked the grid on the burn site at least a hundred times. The DA's going to have a mountain of evidence for the grand jury, the register for which will be copied to me but not for another four or five days, so I won't know until then exactly what they've got on you. In any case, I can almost guarantee they'll hand down an indictment, which means you're back in jail until your trial. Now, what can you tell me?"

"Nothing. I swear, my mind's a blank."

"Who's Desiree?"

Your name numbs me like an animal dart and drops my thoughts in their tracks.

"I don't know."

"You keep saying that. You're not helping. 'Desiree. Goddamn you, Desiree.'" He reads from a photocopy, his voice monotone. "Ring any bells?"

My pulse races and I feel squirming beneath my bandages like a swarm of larvae is hatching under my grafts. There isn't a damned thing I can do except wait for them to scar.

"You've got a week, then, maybe," he says, repacking his files. "Your best move is to make an offer of cooperation. I need to hand them as much information as you can give me, who you were working for, your distributors, your suppliers, everything. Otherwise, get used to your surroundings for the next couple of decades. If I can't make them an offer before your trial, nothing you remember once the trial starts will help." As he stands up he says, "Snap out of it," then drops a business card into my lap. "I'll be in touch."

"Hang on," I say, then I'm blank. The thought flutters out, circles the overhead light in a long silence before it flies back into my head.

"Where will I go when I'm out?"

He's quiet. I stare down at my forearm. The bandages on my back are damp from the seepage through the mesh beneath them. For a moment, I forget I'm not alone in my cell.

"I look like a travel agent to you?" He leans into my face. "You see a name tag on me? There a poster of the Caribbean on the wall?" He's barking too quickly for me to say anything and it hurts to shake my head so I stare at my forearm again.

"You've got a good chunk of cash with your property envelope. I'm sure you'll get by, just don't be too frugal. Enjoy your five days of freedom."

He raps on my cell door and the noise makes me twitch. A buzzer sounds and the door swings open.

"Check my card," he says, stepping out. "The name is 'Morell.' That's me, since you didn't ask. In the future, make sure you know who you're talking to. Call me when you settle in somewhere."

The guard slams my cell door shut and my heart skips. Morell's footsteps recede into the din of buzzing doors that sound like the electric flies in my head swarming to the surging lights of my memory. They're tireless, but if I let them exhaust themselves, they might collapse into a pattern, forming some code in their scattered husks. I stare at my hands for an hour, hoping for a read on my age. If the steel mirror above the toilet is accurate, I'm a human blur. My mug shot is the foggy outline of a nondescript face.

A nightstick thunderclap against my cell door jolts me out of my knuckle and mirror speculation. A paper plate wrapped in cellophane slides through a waist-level opening. Four fish sticks, a biscuit, a plastic fruit cup and a carton of juice, shrink-wrapped at room temperature. The odor slaps me like the ass end of a summer garbage truck when I tear the plastic away. I flush the fish sticks and breathe into the crook of my elbow until my dry heaves stop. The biscuit and warm juice calm my stomach.

I stare at the white walls and try to remember something beyond the preceding seconds spent staring at the infinite white cement in front of me and the cement staring back. I log those seconds into my diary and hope for more.

THE SCHNAUZER BET IT ALL ON A BLUFF BUT THE BULLDOG ISN'T FALLING FOR it. The terrier and the Doberman have folded and all four act like they don't notice me, sitting stock still so I won't notice them. They come down from the walls, along with the black velvet clowns. I run my fingers over the unfaded patches of wallpaper, feeling for holes and tapping for hollow spots, checking the picture frames, lightbulbs, lamp stand, air vents, bed frame and night table for wires. I square off with the big-eyed, frowning circus hobos, scanning for microphones and microlenses. I plug the lamp in eight times, testing for juice socket by socket. Two come up dead. I unscrew the faceplates with a dime but find nothing.

My new cell is room 621 at the Hotel Firebird, a place too much like jail for me to believe I'm out. The hotel warden wears a T-shirt declaring his Vietnam-veteran status and conducts his business through a till inside a chain-link enclosure. Behind him, a massive ring of keys hangs from a nail above a stained baseball bat with "911" carved along its side. Above a small television, a sign reads: "No Visitors After 10 pm, No Loitering in Front, No Change for Vending Machines, Cash Only, No Exceptions."

The residents are a mixture of men and women, recovering and relapsing addicts, and those squarely between either distinction. Some of the doors never open, others never close, the dealers and prostitutes working 24-7 for a piece of business or a piece of a mark, some runaway fresh from the bus station. The hallway lights have burned out; I navigate by the blue glow humming from beneath the doors.

My room has a sink in the corner, a bed, a night table and a small desk with a black-and-white television, a Bible, a deck of cards, a bar of soap, and the stench of every other resident who ignored the soap. Unlike jail, it has a window with a view of the street below. I open the window to let the fresh air in and the human stink out. Looking down to the sidewalk three stories beneath me, I hear an impulse whisper, "jump." I stand still, let my arms go slack to hear the whisper again, then pull myself inside.

I sit on my bed with a game of solitaire spread in front of me. I know the rules but don't remember learning them. The columns of faces and numbers make my head hurt and my bandages itch with static. My notebook awaits the next lucid replay of forgotten seconds, which have felt seconds away for the last hour. A slam of thunder sends the seven of clubs flying. My heart pounds heat to my bandages and blood flares into my new skin. With no forewarning footfalls, a polite knock is a pounding fist is a door crashing to the floor amid airborne hinges and frame splinters, storm troopers storming in from the dark, black armored bugmen aiming laser-guided stingers at my chest, awaiting the queen's orders over the wires lodged in their ears.

This time, it's only a knock. I'm face to face with a pair of Firebird residents who could just as easily need to borrow my soap as kill me.

"Do you have a tapeworm?" His words are soft, the beats measured like the pendulum swing of a pocket watch.

"No. Why would I?"

"Something you ate," he says. His eyes meet the air to the left of mine as though he's reading from cards over my shoulder. "Or the Man has you by the short hair of your balls. Or you're on his payroll."

He dips his chin toward his companion, a lanky stalk of a man over six feet with a tangle of greasy hair hanging below his shoulders. His face is the color of a nicotine stain and he has the blank, bloodless eyes of an old photograph, eyes held too still for too long and frozen onto a silver plate the instant after the flash pan sucked the soul from behind them.

"He can smell tapeworms. He thinks you might be a carrier. Happens sometimes with a new resident."

His companion remains silent. He wears a knee-length black raincoat, oblivious to the evening heat. He could be stretched across a set of crossbeams in a cornfield as easily as he could be flesh and blood.

"Your friend is wrong."

I start to close the door when he says, "My name's Jack." He extends his hand through the opening and his beefy grip swallows mine whole. His palm is slippery with the accumulated grime of a life spent neither working nor washing. When he lets go, his companion has stepped into my room and Jack follows.

His silent friend hisses through clenched teeth and slices a finger across his throat, Quiet. He turns my television on to a dead channel and a canopy of white static deafens any long-range listening. The hissing flickerstorm on-screen envelops me. My heart swells as though I'm listening to an orchestra.

"It's like music," says Jack. "The static is hundreds of millions of years old. It's been flying through space since before time. Remnants of the big bang are strains from the symphony at the beginning of the universe." He smiles and says, "I like to read," then untucks his shirt. "I'm going to show you I'm clean. No tapeworm. No one is listening."

"I don't care. You need to get out."

"If you don't care, then you are most definitely wired."

Jack hikes up his shirt and shows me his bare torso in a full turn. Something terrible was happening to the Virgin of Guadalupe. She'd been rendered in bruise-colored ink, wrapped around Jack's ribs, but her face, body and aura were shredded by a buckshot blast of sores like cigarette burns, some healed to scabs like dots of rust, the rest abscessed and wet, ringed by swollen red stains of infected skin.

His friend does the same. He hangs his coat on my doorknob and lifts his shirt for a three-hundred-sixty-degree view of his chest and back, a scattering of identical sores across both. The television light behind him glows through his skin like sunlight through a paper window screen. Veins and arteries form a webwork beneath the silhouette of his ribs. The murky pulsing of his heart throbs between dull clouds of lung tissue. He drops his shirt and his shadow on the floor darkens back into place.

"What happened to you guys?"

"Bugs. They're everywhere."

Their rooms are infested. They're being eaten alive but asking about tapeworms. Another memory struggles to take solid form but mudslides apart.

"Well?" Jack is waiting. I lift my shirt and turn a full circle.

"I still don't know what you mean," I tell him.

"People come here to go straight. They won't let us. New residents are sometimes wired with a tapeworm. They move in, ask around for this or that, or maybe someone offers the wrong thing and the Man hears all of it. And somebody goes right back inside. But you're clean."

"I just got out of jail."

"What happened to you?"

"Fire."

"Keep clean and covered. Bugs will lay eggs if they get underneath. Give us a urine sample."

On cue, his companion produces an empty coffee cup. I ask him if he's trying to pass a test.

"No, but somebody, somewhere, is. I connect people with what they want. How about you?"

"I OD'd the same time I got burned."

"Things haven't been going well for you, then?"

"I'm saying I'm not clean. I piss in there and somebody gets violated back to jail, I promise you."

"Then give us a cigarette."

"I don't smoke."

"Five dollars."

"What for?"

He surveys my room.

"Because you have it."

The warden must have rented me one of the Firebird's nicer rooms. It has pictures and a sink.

"And what do I get?"

"You understand, now," Jack says. "Perhaps I can help. What are you looking for?"

"Everything I've done before I woke up in jail. I'll piss into any cup, anytime, and pay you ten bucks for your trouble, if you can deliver. If you can't, get out of here."

"That's hardly necessary," he says as though talking in his sleep. "I come here to say hello. I introduce myself and show you I'm on the level. I give you some words of caution. I ask you for a favor, as a friend, and you abandon all courtesy with me. Did I hit you?"

"Take a walk. Leave."

"Did I hit you? Did I take your memory?"

"Now." They're not moving. "The fuck you waiting for?"

"You said ten dollars to know everything you've done. We had an agreement. I told you, I'm on the level."

One minute passes, then another. No sound but the television hissing. Jack is oblivious to my belligerence, his companion to everything else. The absence of everything prior to the last day succumbs to curiosity and I pay him. Beanpole scribbles into a notebook from his pocket. He tears the page loose and hands it to me.

"There you are," Jack says. "There's a theater downtown. You need to go there."

"Which theater?"

"Twenty blocks from our front door, you'll see it. Next to a bar called Ford's. Go inside and you'll get your memory back. Unplug everything when you return. You can hear the electricity and it's unsettling. If there's anything else I can do to make your stay at the Firebird more pleasant, please don't hesitate to contact me. Godspeed."

Beanpole's penmanship is flawless:

Speak to the Token Man. Ask for Desiree.

four

JAIL MOVES WITH ME, AN INVISIBLE BOX SURROUNDING MY EVERY STEP WITH every tick of the clock. A Mexican man in a brown jacket and a cowboy hat, who hasn't smoked in five blocks, lights a cigarette. A woman waiting at a bus stop refolds a newspaper she hasn't been reading. Someone passes me and I count, one thousand, two thousand, three thousand, before I look back. If they're not watching me, they're watching me. Everyone is the Umbrella Man and he is everyone. Every cough, sneeze, smile and wave means both everything and nothing. The signals are everywhere .

Inside the theater—XXX 24 HOUR LIVE NUDE GIRLS XXX—the sign above a glass cabinet of cast latex body parts reads, "See the Token Man for Change." At the far end of an aisle, beyond row after row of yellow, pink and orange video boxes with nude women smiling for a game show but posing for a doctor, sits the Token Man, an obese ingot of flesh with shiny Elvis hair and a silk shirt covered with palm trees and parrots.

"Something I can help you with?"

"I need change."

"What kind?"

"I need them to stop following me."

The Token Man says nothing. He wears a thick, gold rope around his neck and a gold wristwatch the size of a hubcap.

"I'm here for Desiree." Trying to break the silence, I've only made it longer. The Token Man crosses his arms, the chair beneath him creaking from the slight shift in his weight.

"And who said you'd find Desiree here?"

"Jack and the Beanstalk told me."

After another leaden half-minute passes. He asks for twenty dollars in exchange for four brass coins, each stamped with "XXX" on one side, "$1.00" on the other. I'm about to ask for the rest of my money, but the Token Man doesn't look willing to negotiate. If he's charging his own separate toll across the river to Desiree, I won't negotiate, either.

"Booth number four," he says.

A buzzer sounds and I push through a turnstile behind him.

Booth number four is dark and smells like semen, body odor, pine disinfectant and smoke. I try not to breathe through my nose, and stretch the cuff of my sweatshirt over my bare hand as I slide the latch behind me. I feed a token to a coin meter inside, like the kind hooked to an electric pony outside the supermarket, and a window slides open, flooding booth number four with light from a pink room on the other side.

A topless dancer appears, hips and ribs stretching through her skin and a cigarette hanging from her candy red lips, and she moves, oblivious to the dull rhythm pulsing overhead. She's surrounded by lonely men, consumed with their own want, and she knows it. Their wanting hits the glass while her liquid candy smile passes right through. She slips off her panties as though picking her teeth.

"Desiree?"

"You got something for me, baby?"

There's a piece of paper—Tips—taped beside a slot below the window. I slide a Jackson through. I'm at a bank in Hell. She spins around once, then slides a bindle back through the slot. I want fresh air, a shower. I want to change my bandages and incinerate my old ones.

The coin box beeps. The woman blows me a kiss as the window slides down, shutting out the pink light. Outside the booth, a man waits with a mop and a bucket of water so dark the mop head disappears beneath the turgid gray murk, shimmering with the pink and blue neon overhead.

five

THE WHISPER SAID, "SWALLOW." WHEN THE WHISPER IS GONE, SO IS THE BLUE pill. I tune out my second thoughts with a solitaire game.

Reflective reds and blues shift among the queens, jacks and kings, like sunlight on the skin of some tropical reptile. The black lines float above the colors when I view them straight on, as though cut from the air with a razor. I lie back, staring at the luminous queen of hearts and breathing in the scent of wet asphalt drifting through my window, the smell of summer rain hitting the street.

A hand beneath my shirt, palm pressing my chest. I swing, back-handing air. I look through my curtains and it's not raining. Cloudless desert sky and late afternoon sun. I lie back down. I feel the hand of a lover lulling herself to sleep with my heartbeat.

It's you, Desiree.

I feel your hair draped across my neck, your face and fingers on my chest. Your touch spreads across my skin when I take a deep, slow breath, my body like a cigarette glowing brighter with a long drag. Your hand is small and warm with rough fingertips and soft creases in your palm, dissolving the ache in my chest I didn't know existed until it stopped, an ache I've carried for days, maybe my whole life, and it's gone now. If I could stop the setting sun, I would sit in this minute for days on end.

Blood rushes to my brain. The moths swarm to the warm light.

Your sleeping breath brushes my face and blows the ashes from my memory.

Sky the color of dead flies, an unbroken sheet of clouds carried on a warm wind that smells of electricity and flowers. Sweat on my face, my back, I'm sweltering beneath my Sunday best with a cold glass in my hands. The jangle of ice and the distant crash of thunder like an avalanche.

The moving picture stutters and skips, each passing second more familiar than the previous until the streaming rush of memory smoothes into a contiguous chain of moments with your fingers splayed over my stomach, your body against mine.

Damp grass beneath me. The trunk of a tree, the bark as rough and solid as stone, against my back. I smell pears ripening overhead. The horizon snaps blue and more thunder follows. I count the collapsing seconds between the two while the electric air fills my lungs. I inhale the scent of blooming flowers and the wet lawn beneath me that isn't. I can't see you, but your leg is over mine, our ankles intertwined, and I feel the slow swell and collapse of your body breathing against me.

Glass to my lips, I taste sugar, lemon pulp, distant metal in the tap water and ice cubes. I dip my finger to flick an errant gnat from the surface.

A hot rain starts knocking the velvet white pear blossoms to the ground. Each drop smacks my skin while you're curled against me, as though they're falling through your body and hitting mine. The seconds between the flashing sky and the thunder are gone, a torrent of rain and pear blossom petals washes over me. Beneath my suit, the hair on my arms stands on end. The glass explodes in my hand and the universe turns white.

I'm blind.

I'm staring into the sun, so I look away.

A throng of people in black surround a casket being lowered into the ground. I'm wearing dark glasses but still squinting from the daylight and I'm thirsty, like I could drink all of the rain in the sky. Flowers cover the grave, morning glories in full bloom, their petals dipped in the darkening sky, washing their silken white tips in the blue evening. They feel like velvet ribbons between my fingers, like the ears of a delicate rodent.

Three crude pills in my palm. Gypsies. I made them from the morning glories in my garden. The daylight fades, leaving the heat stranded behind, and the symphony of crickets scores the encroaching dark. The first flicker of the first firefly is the signal to swallow my Gypsies.

Vertigo seizes my stomach. My face boils in anticipation of retching over my porch rail but the nausea snaps away, leaving me alone in the cloudless, moonless night full of stars and fireflies.

Switching off my porch light switches on the sky and I'm suddenly staring into the center of the galaxy. The stars are close enough to cup between my palms and they drift among the trees, shimmering from the silent singing of the bats, whose music hums against my skin. I spot one of their spastic silhouettes the second before it snatches a star out of my reach. The hazy supernova glows through the bat's belly before it fades into a flapping black hole in the darkness and the singing begins again.

The fireflies are trailed by shimmering corkscrews of light. They spin webs among the trees as they move, their threads ending where singing bats snatch the spinners from midair.

One lands on my arm. Another lands on my chest, then another, the dots of light flaring brighter before they fly off, each tethered to me by a rope of frozen lightning, stretching and glowing longer and brighter. The crisscrossing ribbons of light left in their wake fuse into a luminous mesh, surrounding me.

My crying makes the lights brighter. I can't stop and don't want to. If every link in the chain of life is this beautiful, then I'll die of beauty if I ever see the whole chain at once, joining the chain with my link in its place and the chain stretching from one end of eternity to the next. I'll spend forever staring God in the eye with God staring back.

Beautiful, is all I can think. Beautiful, beautiful, beautiful, beautiful. A small eternity passes and still the word sounds distant and dry, incapable of matching its own meaning.

God's own clock quicksand slows to an ice-whisper quiet. I follow the smell of morning glories, pear blossoms, wet summer grass, sweet lemon and electricity, everything in God's chain braided into a single, warm breeze and the chain leads me to you. Your pale skin shines in the dark, and your hands leave dim tracers when you move, shrouding you in the cloudy embrace of your own ghost a hundred times over. Your hair is the color of thread spun from a flaming wheel.

Couples hold hands, children throw coins into fountains, street performers sing, juggle, twist balloons and walk on glass. Mimes mimic the unwitting, women braid hair and paint children's faces. A shirtless young man wearing fatigues and a rigid, black mohawk, a crushed hat full of money at his feet, juggles torches, stopping to hold one aloft and spit a cloud of fire into the air. A hundred feet from him, a blond boy, no more than sixteen or seventeen, squirms and writhes his way from a straitjacket.

Between the fire-breather and the escape artist, you sit on the stone edge of a fountain, a paisley kerchief draped over a folding table no wider than a bar stool in front of you.

"Tell your fortune?"

"My fortune's very good, right now. Thank you."

You reach for my hand. Yours are dry and cracked, with long nails painted the color of dried blood, an old woman's hands with a young woman's face.

"You almost died when you were a boy. You were sitting beneath a tree when it was hit by lightning."

You don't know my name, but you know the exploding glass and pear-blossom-petal rain by the lines in my hand.

"How do you know that?"

You don't answer. You run the tip of your blood-colored nail over my palm.

"They thought you might have heart trouble as you got older, but you're fine." You seat me beside you on the fountain. "You're superstitious around trees, though. Loud noises startle you and you're always thirsty. It never goes away."

"And my future? Can you see that?"

"You're drunk."

"I'm not drunk. Not exactly. Tell me more."

You squint, holding my palm up to the lights.

"Your parents were very religious. You lost one of them, one you were close to."

"You're slipping," I say. "That's vague."

"It was your father. You were close to him and he died soon after your accident."

*

Dad told me he could make the stars bleed. He set his tripod in our yard one summer night. We shared soda from a cooler and popcorn from an aluminum stew pot. The stars and the fireflies were our only light, the crickets and our breathing the only sound. Dad smelled like barbershop aftershave and developing fluid. He asked if I wanted to take a picture of my own and I did.

I clicked open the camera shutter and a white wire of light shot across the sky, crumbled into sparks and vanished. Will that be in the picture, I asked, and Dad said yes.

The lightning bugs blinked in the heat like constellations mirrored in rippling water. Could you take a picture of them, I asked. Dad said he'd help me take one myself.

I liked working in the red glow of Dad's darkroom. He'd converted our storm cellar into a photo lab with safety lights and storage for his emulsions and fixers. The darkroom was our lone surviving father-and-son project. The last thing we'd built together, before that, was a radio from a spool of copper wire and a crystal. I thought we'd need tubes and a bulky wooden housing but dad said no, the signals are everywhere, you just need to listen. The remnants of that project lay in a box beside a stack of magazines, collecting dust. *The signals are everywhere.* I can almost hear his voice.

We worked together, Dad transferring the prints between pans while I rinsed and clipped them to the drying line. The stars shone brighter in his pictures than in life. Dad took long exposures of the sky, and the stars bled in perfect arcs that made me dizzy, as though Dad had photographed the very spinning of the earth. I found my picture, marked by the white slash and hazy burst where the comet had vanished.

The firefly pictures had trails that quivered like an old person's handwriting and, wherever they had stayed in one spot for more than a second, bright stains leaked onto the film like car headlights in a heavy rain. The trails stopped and started midair wherever the bugs had blinked off for a moment. I lost myself under the red lights, following the erratic path of a single firefly through its glowing labyrinth, the electric spiderweb twisted in a fun house mirror.

I'd forgotten about that.

"I've stepped into that picture," I said. "What do I owe you?"

"Whatever you feel your memory is worth." Trails streak from your necklace, from the children running with glow sticks around the fountain.

I empty my pockets into your cigar box.

"Are you here tomorrow?"

"Maybe."

"I thought you could tell the future."

"Would you still come looking for me, even if you weren't certain I'd be here?"

"Yes. I would."

"Then look for me tomorrow. Maybe you'll find me."

A dog jumps from the fountain and the children squeal. Beneath a streetlight, he shakes himself dry in a furious, spastic blast of water. The explosion of drops lit from above looks like the birth of the universe, like a hundred million fireflies hatched in the same half second and blown from the nest, fully grown. A man laughs uncontrollably, wiping the pinpoint flames from his glasses, brushing them from his blond hair, and they cascade to the sidewalk like a shower of welding sparks. The sight leaves me weak.

The man puts his glasses on and I wonder, does he know he's been kissed by the beginning of the universe.

"That's Otto," you said.

Hello, Otto.

"And I'm Eric." I give you my hand one more time.

"Lovely meeting you, Eric." The silver wires of your bracelets throw splinters of light into the air when you take my hand.

"I'm Desiree."

Your whisper brushes my ear. I wrap my arms around you, but you're gone. Your fingers slip from around my heart, your ghost fades from my bed.

After my heart has bloomed to the size of the universe and all the love from the big bang to the last whisper has been cycloning through my chest for what feels like days on end, the world is one giant prison when the storm dies, at last. The galaxies shrink back to the lump of muscle behind my ribs, the sniper's target just to the left of my spine. The sleepless night and following day weigh down like a leaden, gray forever. It feels like dying.

I thought I missed you, Desiree. I had no idea how much.

six

THE WRONG MOVE WILL SPLIT MY SKIN DOWN THE CENTER OF MY BODY.
It will fall away in sheets like brittle, peeling paint. My eyes scrape their
sockets and I hear sounds like a shrieking chalkboard when I blink. I lie
motionless, but feel motion sick.

A sting to my inner thigh. I fling the sheets away and jump to my
feet. The room spins. I think it's in my head, then I think not. I close my
eyes and it's worse. Faster, faster. Ground impact will blow out the windows, collapse the ceiling and scatter my shattered bones and furniture
like God flinging a handful of dice. I brace myself but the spinning slows.
I hold my balance against the wall, scratching the fresh welt on my leg.

On hands and knees at bug level for the second time. Either I
missed this one or it's new, or whatever infested Jack's room has hitch-
hiked on his dumpster-salvaged wardrobe and shat its eggs into my
carpet and sheets. Smaller than my thumb and the color of its own
shadow, it disappears into the mottled carpet beside the lamp cord like
the splatter fragment of an old stain. Anslinger's black-bag men had
planted it in plain sight.

It senses movement and bolts for the corner. I trap it beneath the
empty jar and slide the queen of hearts beneath it. It looks like a
smooth, black stone flailing in vain at the invisible wall.

Cuts and burns scar the desk. They're the handiwork of the desperate
and industrious armed with razors, spoons, glass pipes and butane

lighters. In the drawer, they've left behind a rubber band, two thumbtacks, a dried-out ballpoint pen with no cap, a few paperclips and a dull razorblade. I pull the jar away and the specimen runs for the edge, but I flip it onto its back with the queen of hearts. In spite of my hangover, my hands are steady and I pin it through the center with a straightened paperclip on my first try.

Its antennae hum, black filaments longer than its entire body, a signal for help or a last-ditch attempt to relay its gathered data back to the colony. I tap them at the base with the razorblade, severing the connection.

Across town, the detective's monitor cuts to a bug's-eye view of the big bang, and the blowtorch hiss of static.

Fuck you, Anslinger.

The head remains intact until I can find out what it's seen and heard, though I may have punctured its microprocessor. I peel its wings from beneath as it struggles. I can scarcely imagine the electric insect invective it's hurling at me from its dying, foul bug mouth. I disassemble it leg by leg, wing by wing. I break its shell into its core components, bisect its head and cross section its body four times but have nothing to show for my work. Nothing shorts, nothing sparks and nothing smokes. No resistors or transistors. No crystals, diodes, coils or microchips, only moist entrails. Whoever made this is good, so they were smart enough to make others.

Umbrella Men wave down buses and speak into pay phones. They fold newspapers and hold radios to their ears. Anslinger is tracking me. Anslinger wants to send me back to jail. Anslinger isn't interested in me, he wants Desiree. He wants my Desiree. He's looking for the Glass Stripper. All or none of the above. I ditch one scenario in favor of another between footsteps. I check reflections in shop windows and bus shelters. Some kid bends to tie his shoe. Left foot means, We've been made, pull back. Right foot means, Go, to the rooftop sniper with the laser dot firefly humming on the back of my head, awaiting his signal to pull the trigger and turn off the universe.

The sign says FORD'S. Floodlights illuminate BEER-POOL-SATELLITE TV on the outside wall. Inside, the carpet might be gray, green or black. The scant light is of scant help in determining anything. Stains on the pool table, maybe beer, maybe blood. A jukebox with "Out of Order" taped over the glass. The bartender's shirt has "Lou" embroidered onto the chest.

"I guess you're Lou."

He's wiping a glass with a gray towel, staring at my face like he's just scraped me off his shoe.

"Have I been here before?"

"If you don't know, then it's time to quit," he says. "What can I get you?"

I don't know.

"The usual."

Stock cars race through a haze of electric snow on the silent television mounted above the bar. Pool balls crack against each other on the beer-and-blood stained table behind me. Lou remains inert, determined to wipe the reflections off the glass with that gray towel. My hands shake. Something lands on my face and I slap my cheek, expecting a splattered bug on my fingers. Nothing but the shine of sweat, more running down my temples and neck. I pull a ten from my pocket, so Lou serves me instead of tossing me out.

"Jack and Coke," he says. "Good beginner's drink."

Other customers have red and black coasters beneath their drinks. Lou sets my glass down on the bare wood, the glass hits with a cracking noise like a fast pool shot. He resumes polishing with the soiled towel.

"There a pay phone here?"

Lou responds with a jut of his chin. Toward the back. A sign points down a small hallway, RESTROOMS AND PHONE.

Anslinger's direct line dumps me to his machine.

"Call off your tail. I'm doing the best I can, but stop following me. And stop bugging my room." Before hanging up, I pause and add, "Please."

Someone behind me says, "You've looked better, Eric."

I strain to picture this man. I remember his clothes, khaki trousers and a peach golf shirt, but not his face. He's with a boy dressed in a shirt stained like a shop rag and a blue windbreaker a size too large. Scabs like playground injuries stipple the bridge of his runny nose, his hair is matted as though he'd fallen asleep in the dirt. He stares at his fingers, silently moving his lips. Not a boy, but a year or two within my age. I saw him earlier, tying his shoe on the sidewalk.

The unmemorable man touches the boy gently on the back as he passes me on his way to the men's room.

"Have we met?"

"You don't recognize me?" he asks.

I strain to move the blood through my head, so the heat and light will coax a memory out of hiding. The bar lights surge and the jaws of an electric dog clamp onto my back ribs. I see storm clouds and smell pear blossoms for a heartbeat before my knees turn to wax.

On my back. Turning over but my legs won't move. My arms tingle and burn like they're asleep. Need to watch for the shattered lemonade glass. Trying to crane my neck. All I can see are the man's shoes and shins. Spit hangs from my lips. I can't keep from drooling, and the shoes look expensive so I need to be careful.

"How about now?" he says.

The tingling in my arms rages with a second surge from the dog's teeth. I hear a thunderclap and feel the first drops of hot rain on my face before I collapse again onto wet grass, the chrome leg of the pinball machine the only thing in my field of view. I smell summer, dirt, popcorn from the bar, the stench from the toilets, stale smoke, pear blossoms, lemonade, smoking bark, my own cooked and blistered skin, then nothing.

seven

GRASS STABS MY NOSTRILS AND EYES AS RAIN SLIDES DOWN MY CHEEKS. THE drops climb through my hair and ears, foraging beneath my collar. It's not raining. Beetles swarm from the dirt and pick me apart, scrambling for the precious patches of thin skin, fighting for the wet tissue inside my mouth and beneath my bandages. Antenna codes rebound from drone to drone in the space of a wing flutter until the machine-forged workers deep down catch the signal. The six-legged drill bits burrow up through the dirt to pick my cartilage clean with surgical steel mandibles until nothing's left but my brittle bones for the hot rain to hammer into the mud. You say my name, your voice muffled with static. Flash. One thousand, two thousand, three thousand. Thunder. Wiggle your toes. I don't have any. Other people have toes, I have shoes. Wiggle your shoelaces. Nothing. I can't run from the legions of whoever or whatever are charging through the splintered door I can't see. Open your eyes.

I'm buckled into the passenger seat of a minivan. The stranger in the peach golf shirt is driving.

"That's what we call a Simi Valley speeding ticket." He reaches for my face. With his thumb on my cheek, he stretches my left eye wide open. "You there?" He lets go of my face and takes the wheel. "The question is," he says, "can you do it again?"

My fingers crackle. My motor control thaws as I rub my palms together. A voice behind shouts for ice cream, a child's plea coming from a grown man.

"We're going to get some ice cream right now, son," the driver says. Then to me, "What happened to the hard-ass I used to know? Only a couple of weeks ago you were pure brains and attitude. Now, you're a shivering wreck."

The taste of metal lingers. My tongue won't move and I can't swallow. I might choke on my own spit. The windows are up, the air conditioner blows the faint lemon and pear blossom smells away with cold, empty air.

"Ice cream."

"Settle down, son."

Wherever I am, it's far from the Firebird's part of town. We drive among the houses I've seen in the distance from my window, box-shaped insect hives the color of sand, with red tile roofs behind high walls or iron fences. They cover the hills like barnacles. The Summit. Shady Pointe. Vista Acres. Groups of Mexican men trim hedges and lawns every half mile. The brightest color is the manicured grass that's never seen a picnic blanket, lawn chair or baseball game. I don't smell anything.

"I'm sorry about the shock," the man says. "My son likes his toys and I'm a big believer in a strong offense. You used to know that. That's my boy back there. You've met him before, many a time."

He gauges my reaction in silence.

"Nothing, huh?"

Nothing.

"Don't fool yourself," he continues. I'm paralyzed and have to listen. "He knows every major artery, nerve cluster and pressure point on the human body. He can gut, cut and pack a grown man into a garbage bag in under forty minutes. He's still just a child in most ways, always will be. But he's got a knack for the job most pros will never come close to. Ever. He's a legend, in some circles. You're the best, aren't ya, Toe Tag?" he says to the rearview mirror.

"Love you."

"I love you too, son. Here we are."

He pulls into a shopping complex, the same bleached sand non-color of the surrounding developments, and parks in a blue zone. The dirty, idiot boy from Ford's opens my door. Toe Tag. He unbuckles my seat belt, grips the crotch of my arm and hoists me to my feet. I'm a doll full of feathers in his grip.

The evening shadows bleed like fresh ink until they've covered the ground. The desert air soaks them up, staining the sky deep blue, the color of morning glory petals. The sweeping hands of the enormous, outdoor clock make me dizzy. I stare at my feet and let Toe Tag guide me. My legs are still numb and I can't risk slipping on a wet shadow.

My escorts leave me at an outdoor food court opposite a movie theater. I hear the hornet's hum of current running through neon. When they return, the boy plows into a waffle cone, smearing ice cream across his face, oblivious to the world.

"My name is White," the man says. "They call me Manhattan, but I'm from Rochester. I'll repeat myself. The question is, can you do it again?" He strokes his son's hair once, twice, then folds his hands in front of him, never taking his eyes from me.

"You're really going to make me go through this from the beginning, aren't you?"

I still can't talk. Neither shaking my head nor nodding seems like a good idea.

Toe Tag says, "Share," then offers a spoonful of ice cream to his father. Manhattan White lets the boy spoon-feed him a bite, then continues.

"You and I work for the same organization. Rather, we used to, as you've taken an unscheduled leave of absence. Among our interests is a chain of pharmaceutical manufacturing and supply, wherein you reported to me as part of Research and Development. Head of Research and Development, I should add. I reported, and continue to report, directly to Mr. Hoyle."

Toe Tag immerses a plastic army man into his ice cream. Hip-deep in vanilla, the soldier with the seam down the center of his face rears back to lob a grenade into mine.

"That placed you very high up in the chain, you understand," says White. "You've made a great deal of money for us, and yourself, and we've been quite pleased with you, until this recent debacle."

"And to whom does Hoyle report?" A rope of drool spills onto my numb and tingling hands. I wipe my chin with unfeeling fingers.

"This is going to take longer than I thought," says White. "Hoyle reports to no one. He's the first and last link in the chain and everything in it belongs to him. He's the last word in this organization, his organization, and you've managed to land on his blacklist. Most people would have been given a pink slip in your situation, but you've got yourself one hell of a parachute, so we're prepared to negotiate."

"You've got my undivided attention." My words are mashed together like warm clay.

"Sarcasm. Sounds as though the old Eric is coming around," he says and smiles. "There's that fire you started. That is not an accusation, so we're clear. Neither I nor Hoyle believe you did that on purpose. Your precautionary measures were exemplary for the entire chain and your compensation was ample, to say the very least. Nobody doubts it was an accident but, the fact remains, the lab was your responsibility and the fire happened on your watch."

"Hoyle ought to be insured."

"He is and he isn't," White says, "but it's not that simple. In addition to the significant loss of our assets, both manufacturing and finished product, there's the question of some intellectual property, work you did for hire, which therefore belongs to us, and lastly, there's reason to believe, and I'm being generous here, that you were personally responsible for inventory shrinkage at the site. Now with your legal situation, we face the potential compromise of your Nondisclosure Agreement with the organization. This poses the most significant danger to Hoyle, which thus poses the most significant danger to you."

"Is that a threat?"

"Yes. Would you like it in writing?"

"I haven't said a thing to the cops."

"But they've asked."

"I didn't answer."

"I know you didn't," says White. "Otherwise Toe Tag here would have issued you a severance package. But they've asked nonetheless, and will continue to ask, as will they continue to barter your future in exchange for a violation of your Nondisclosure."

I dig my nails into my palms and bite my lower lip until the pain punches through the static.

"I can't barter with what I don't know, and I don't know anything." My words are solid and clear. I scrape my tongue across my teeth and force sensation to return. I taste blood.

"You're right, I probably was responsible for shrinkage because I've done some serious damage to my brain, so you can forget about my saying anything. I'm guessing Hoyle can't use the fire as a tax write-off, if I'm hearing you correctly. And I'm in no position to compensate Hoyle or the chain for the damage you say I'm accountable for."

"The police are saying it as well, so I don't think that issue's in dispute."

"Right. So what are you and I discussing?"

"One of two things," White says. "First, you say you're unprepared to compensate for the loss of the lab, but you're mistaken. You were one of our highest-salaried nonexecutives. You were also a workaholic with a modest lifestyle. So, it's fair to assume that you are, in fact, capable of compensating for the damage. We're prepared to wait until you've recovered from the incident in the desert and can access whatever offshore accounts or storage units you've invested your earnings in."

"And if I can't?"

"There's the matter of some research and development. Again, you're in possession of some intellectual property of ours."

"I'm not in possession of intellectual anything." My spit tastes like I've been drinking from a metal can. The electric numbness gives way to a fire beneath my bandages. If I hurt them when I collapsed, the skin grafts might not take.

"I've known you for a while, Eric. I have faith in you." He stands and, without a word, Toe Tag once again helps me to my feet.

"Nonetheless, in your present state, your Nondisclosure Agreement remains uncompromised. It's my job to see that, as your mental condition improves, you're able to solve our issue of compensation while maintaining the integrity of our trade secrets."

"What's my job?"

"Remember. And keep your mouth shut."

"That's exactly what the cops, and my lawyer, said. You'd all get along. Want me to introduce you?"

"Once more, I see the old Eric coming through. Trust me, this will work itself out sooner than you think."

"I need to get back." I never made it to the Glass Stripper.

"Where's back?"

Whether Anslinger's tailing me or White, I don't want them dropping me at the hotel.

We drive in silence. Moths cluster against the streetlamps, throwing shadows the size of vultures against the stucco fortress walls protecting Shady Pointe and Vista Acres. The anthill houses are all the same color of dark once the sun has set. White never looks at me or at his son. If Toe Tag is awake, he's studying the back of my head.

"Here you are," White says. I said anywhere, so he drops me back at Ford's. "Let's grab a latte some time."

eight

MEMORIES SWARM TO THE BRIGHT POINT BURNING IN THE DARK LIKE A SHELL of dust around a dying star. I see patterns in the formation, gaps between the humming wings and antennae. The code in the patterns is as real as your skin pressed next to mine, and the code tells me I'm a boy again.

I've doubled my hit from yesterday, bracing myself to fall from the sky in flames when the rush wears off, but it's worth it to feel your arms coiled around my chest, your nose and lips pressed to my neck. It's worth it to feel the kiss of the universe surging from my stomach, up through my heart and down through my legs.

Jack was right, I can hear the current in the wires. I've unplugged the lamps and unscrewed every bulb, but the currents hum like an angry locust trapped in my ears. I can walk my room blindfolded, guided by the drone of the currents and the taste of rancid tin. I stuff a towel beneath my door and cover the wall sockets with pillows, but the sounds intrude the way a leaking pipe taps through my sleep.

I bought a piece of God, ground to dust and mixed with alcohol in a glass bottle the color of molasses. It said "Poison" above the red skull and crossbones, and "Arsenic" below.

"Rat shit." Dad crouched on the floor of our cellar darkroom, pinching a bead like soft, brown clay between his thumb and forefinger.

I heard them during the night, the scratch of their claws and the drag of their tails like leather ropes across our roof. We dripped arsenic onto sugar cubes and smeared seltzer tablets with peanut butter. We planted the bait in pie tins on our roof and in our cellar. Some rats ate the tainted sugar, others ate the peanut butter and ruptured from the inside, their innards swelling out of their dead, gaping mouths. I experimented on my own, my curiosity leapfrogging from combining different poisons to new methods of disguising bait. Arsenic, I learned, was an element, one of ninety-eight atoms composing the entire universe. God, I reasoned, was part arsenic. That part of God killed vermin and sent people into convulsions.

While other kids my age mowed lawns or delivered newspapers, I shoveled hairy lumps of meat from our rooftop and cellar. Storm season had arrived and Mom was terrified of being trapped underground with a single rat, dead or alive, much less a colony.

Dad taught me about the sirens. My job was to open every window in our house when they sounded, and to keep the outside entrance to the storm cellar unlocked. Each second between the sky's flash, one thousand, two thousand, three thousand, and the thunder equaled one mile between you and the wrath of God, and God was nothing if not faster than your change of heart. He could be flooding the next county or burning the next state then, six thousand, three thousand, one thousand, before you can slide the deadbolt shut and whisper for mercy, His dogs are on you.

You haven't heard loud until you've heard God's jackbooted angels kicking down the door to the sky, ripping yours from its hinges and your house from its foundation. Angels don't knock or ask for paperwork. They cleave the biggest tree on your property down the middle, blow your fuses, smoke your television, radio and phone lines and leave you for dead.

Sometimes thunder sounded that wasn't thunder, but a slamming door that made the windowpanes, drywall and picture frames shudder. Mom and Dad never shouted or raised their voices. Anger was a sin. If they didn't shout, it wasn't anger. Being drunk was a sin. Drinking was not. Having a drink doesn't make you a drunk, Mom said. So they drank in secret, each of them hiding it from the other. Following an afternoon of clandestine drinking, they'd be not drunk and not fighting. They hissed through clenched teeth and flaring neck veins. The wrong question, Where's Dad, What's for dinner, Can I watch TV, tripped the tension wire. The explosion with a belt or wooden spoon wasn't anger, but discipline, so it wasn't a sin, either.

The force and volume of routine activity marked the tension, whether food was served or slapped onto plates, dishes stacked or dishes dropped. The tapping and scraping of silverware were the only sounds during a wordless meal. Their rage was as tangible as a change in the weather. Between the clatter of the coffeepot and the descending silence I counted, one thousand, two thousand, three thousand, before a door slammed or a plate exploded without a word. I glazed shattered windowpanes, spackled walls and hung doors without being asked, complicit in whitewashing the quiet hate crushing our house.

In the red glow of the storm cellar, Dad and I heard the sirens. I ran upstairs, opened the windows and grabbed my radio. Dad was gone when I returned. I heaved open the doors leading outside, hail stinging my face and my ears popping, calling for Dad. My voice was a whisper buried in the roar, the sound of a train engine all around me.

Dad stood, snapping pictures beside the pear tree in our yard, ignoring the sirens, the wind, hail and sound of the roaring train. In the distance, a chunk of the sky came loose and fell groundward, dragging the rest of the sky behind. It hit the earth like an enormous black spike, and I saw a house vanish in a puff of splinters. The black spike twisted and squirmed, the sky fighting to pull it back into place. It fought back. It threw mailboxes, dogs and doors, anything and everything, to keep hold of the ground. Dad finally waved me downstairs, then followed.

We crouched in our red and ratless storm cellar darkroom while God, all of God's dogs and God's biggest, fiercest angels kicked and screamed from outside. They tore the inside of our house to pieces and threatened to crush the house itself. They kicked in the doors, snapping them from their frames. They hammered at the rusty deadbolt on the outside entrance and they howled and shrieked at us to open up, raining concrete dust onto our heads, spitting hail through the cracks in our basement. The red lights flared on, then off, then exploded in a rain of white sparks. We couldn't hear our own voices over their screaming but we never moved, we never let them in.

nine

DEBRIS RAINS INTO MY EYES. I TRY TO PICK THEM CLEAN BUT FIND NOTHING.

The house isn't shaking and God isn't kicking the door down. I'm at the Firebird. The shower of dirt is a hive of phantom bugs picking at my skin with a million invisible mandibles. Someone swapped my skull for another during the night. It's too big for my face, but too tight for my brain. The bones in my shoulders, elbows and knees vibrate within my muscles like rusty hinges. I drink from the tap until my stomach can't hold any more, but my throat is still packed with cotton, my bandages stuffed with sawdust.

Shaving might as well be eye surgery, my hands quivering like they are. Something darts across my bare foot. Tiny claws and a pink leather tail. Spinal chills kick the phantom mandibles into overdrive. My hand slips and my razor drops into the sink, a layer of spent foam, wet stubble and fresh blood.

They've chewed through the damp baseboard beneath the sink. I grab a pair of dirty socks and stuff one into the rat hole and mop my bloody chin with the other.

Jack and the Beanstalk sit together like an old couple. Jack reads a newspaper. Beanstalk sits transfixed by the television static, a pair of headphones clamped to his ears.

"You're in love, aren't you?" Jack doesn't look up from his paper.

I dig change from my pockets for the coffee machine. Maybe Jack catches me staring at his friend.

"He hasn't spoken since Miles Davis died," he says.

The coffee machine drones like an earth mover.

"You can't be troubled," says Jack. "I understand."

A cardboard specimen cup drops from the chute, followed by a hot trickle.

"Did you find Desiree?" His paper is years out of date. The front page announces a U.S.-launched missile attack against Libya.

"Yeah, thanks."

"And you're in love. Am I right or not?"

"Sure. Sort of."

"Of course you are. You reek of it." He folds his newspaper, slowly and deliberately, so someone else can read about the manhunt for Gadhafi.

"It's beautiful," he says, "every time is like the first. There's nothing like it."

"Right."

"And the currents?" The same patronizing, metronome voice. "Are they a menace, or simply a nuisance?"

The coffee tastes like dishwater boiled in a discarded tire.

"You don't realize what's inside the walls until you can hear it," Jack says. "Miles of wire, humming with current. Power lines, transformers, radio waves, microwaves, radar. Do you have any metal fillings?"

"I don't know, I haven't checked."

"Keep your vigil or those transmissions unravel inside your ears. You hear every phone conversation, talk show and radio jingle all at the same time and you can't turn them off. It's like being a god, omniscient and insane, both at once. That kind of love will drive you mad."

"I'll be careful."

"Careful is for tourists. You're trespassing on too late. You've already said you're in love."

"I'll pick up some foil, make a beanie. Tell me your hat size and I'll kick one your way. Will that help?"

"No, it will not. Nor will your sarcasm and lack of courtesy."

"I need to get going."

"I'm trying to help you, 621. Anything you haven't remembered yet, you forgot for a reason. Cut her loose. The heartache will be nothing compared to the noise in your head, if you do it now."

I'm out the door when he shouts, "I'm the only friend you've got."

What they call a gown is a paper bib the color of toilet cleaner that hangs to my knees. The first nurse weighs me, the second takes my blood pressure and a third listens to my heart. The fourth asks about the medicines I'm supposed to be taking but haven't been. I imagine they build igloos or chisel ice sculptures between patients, and they mark the same clipboard and say the doctor will be with me soon. Two minutes each, over two hours.

A girl lies opposite me, a tube in her arm and another in her nose. The bandages around her head dip to cover her left eye. A woman sits with her beside a small beeping box and holds her hand. Near a fire extinguisher lies a man on a gurney. He is either homeless or dead, or both. Blood from his face and chest soaks through the sheets, growing darker and duller as I watch. They'll have to be torn from his skin.

We're in full view of the hospital staff, our bandages, blood and paper bibs, yet we're invisible. The great antidrama of life among the stucco hives in the hills above the Firebird unfolds while we wait. Someone got engaged or spent the weekend away at a wedding, or a funeral. Someone lost money on a game, colored her hair, got his car out of impound or got laid. Someone applied to graduate school or drank too much. The mundane details both impossible and unreal compared to my last forty-eight hours.

The Hotel Firebird stinks with the fumes of humanity packed into a brick box, churning out piss, sweat, cum and blood, the liquid of living things. Houses the color of prosthetic limbs, nestled within the calibrated green hills of Shady Pointe, filter and flush that cocktail of stench with extreme prejudice. The odorless nothing I smelled in those hills and at the mall was nothing, neither foul nor antiseptic, but nothing nonetheless. I know, because the smell of nothing is all around here. Every measure is taken to discharge and disguise the smells and secretions of the living struggling for life. Death waits, bobbing in a sealed jar of formaldehyde as half the life here is half naked and wholly alone, ignored by the other half wearing pale green scrubs and living in muted brown homes.

Dr. Stanley examines me without making eye contact. He speaks to the clipboard or to my bandages.

"I see you're in much better shape than when I last saw you." He's four years older than me, at most. His Adam's apple distends like a mop handle pushing through the back of his neck.

"How are you feeling?"

"I'm cold."

There's a curtain to my left, two men talking behind it. One uses his voice for the first time since Death sang him to sleep and a medic slapped him awake, exhuming his rusted throat from the mud and weeds. The voice asks to be discharged.

"It says here your temperature is normal." Dr. Stanley reads from the communal clipboard. "Fever or chills could be a signal of complications. How long have you been feeling cold?"

"Since I've been sitting here in my underwear waiting for you."

He doesn't say anything. His Adam's apple plunges the length of his neck when he swallows.

An orderly steps from behind the curtain. He's enormous, his skin so dark it shines blue where the light hits it. He fills a paper cup from a drinking fountain and says to the voice, "You'll be discharged following an interview with another doctor." The voice says, "It was an accident, I don't need to see another doctor."

Dr. Stanley inspects my bandages.

"They itch," I tell him, "and I'm coughing a lot."

"There's early signs of infection," he says. "That's not good. After we redress these, I'm putting you on a stronger antibiotic regimen."

"I'm on one now?"

"That might be the problem. Are you getting enough liquids?"

"What's enough?"

"Eric, you're risking a rejection of the skin grafts. Lay off the alcohol, drink more water. Burns like this one disrupt the fluid balance in your tissue. Go easy on yourself. How are you otherwise? Is your memory improving?"

"Some. Hard to say."

Big nurse says to the voice, "It's not up to me. We have to report this sort of thing. Sit tight."

The voice asks for coffee.

Dr. Stanley writes me a scrip for steroids, a fresh battery of antibiotics and painkillers.

Mirrored blisters swell from the ceiling where the cameras hide. I didn't see them the other day. I stare too long at the overhead chrome, frozen midboil, and the room goes liquid. The gray bucket mop man's roiling floor tiles throw my footing and I knock a display to the floor, a chaotic collage of naked women and tropical beaches, a fusion of a travel brochure and medical textbook.

"You need some help?"

I've disturbed the Token Man.

"I was here yesterday."

"Let me punch your card. Your tenth show is free."

I have no idea what he's talking about.

"I didn't get a card."

The Token Man's shirt could have come from a queen-sized bedsheet. He pauses in the split moment before giving me the business end of whatever problem solver he's stashed beneath the counter. His eyes are on me like sniper dots and the chrome blisters log my every twitch. Antennae tickle my neck and ears. At first, I think it's sweat until the bugs lose their grip and drop down my shirt and struggle to climb out the top of my jeans. I stoop to gather the video boxes, to keep from slapping myself in a frenzy.

"Don't worry about 'em," he says.

"It's no problem."

"Leave 'em alone." He thinks I'm out of my head, but he won't throw me out. He knows I've got money.

"Is Desiree working?"

"Must be, if you're here." He exchanges twenty dollars for four dollars in tokens. "Booth four."

The pinpoint of green light from the pony ride coin box lights booth number four. I drop a token into the box and pull my cash as the looking glass slides open.

"You pull your piece, I pull mine."

Anslinger stands framed and backlit in the pink window with his silver screen slicked-back hair and pinstripe orchid tie. His dress shirt is the same liquid amber of his eyes, his suit a deep green verging on black, with a camel hair coat draped over his arm.

"Come now," he says. "I haven't drawn my gun in two years. You pull anything out and I will shoot you in the belt buckle. Now, what are you doing here?"

The money is a soiled sock in my hand. I want to shrink down and crawl into a crack but not here, not these cracks.

"The doctor needs a sperm sample, but the magazines at the hospital weren't doing it for me. When did you start working here?"

"When did you decide to stop cooperating?" he asks.

"The cockroaches tell you that? You shouldn't listen to them. They're pissed because I'm a neat freak. I moved into that shit-hole room and swept up the crack pipes and bread crumbs. I killed one of them, so the whole colony's got it in for me. It's your colony, so you already know that."

"Where you been, Eric? I've been hearing crickets on my voice mail for two days."

"You know exactly where I've been. Your spies are in my room and crawling through my clothes."

"That's not how I work," says Anslinger. "I don't come to you. You come to me."

"What luck. I just wandered into your office. Or is this where your daughter works?"

Anslinger goes ice water on me, his warm eyes freezing to glass. He's neither angry nor amused. He stares at the center of my forehead, and there's nothing behind it that's any good to him.

"Mention my daughter again."

The pony box timer counts down with the temperature.

"Go on. Mention my daughter."

Voices seep through the walls, moaning with pure pleasure but sounding like near death, obscenities serving as endearments.

"Get a magazine," Anslinger shouts, and hammers the window to his left.

I hear the door bolt open, the hasty departure of a frustrated patron.

"I spoke with your lawyer," he says.

"So you know that I shouldn't even be talking to you."

"I know you're supposed to be cooperating. But he hasn't heard from you, either. In a few days, he's getting a set of binders, all of them thicker than the Old Testament. Every speck of glass we found within a hundred miles of the burn will be listed. We've run toxicity reports on the soil and groundwater. Everything. It's on you. The registration for your car listed the burn site as your address. But guess who owns the place? Guess who's legally responsible for what went down there?"

Maybe White, maybe not.

"We don't know, either," he says. "The deed is held by a limited liability company, represented by a law firm with a private mailbox address in Nevada. The paper trail fades out somewhere in the Cayman Islands."

"I'm not hiding. I'm trying to remember. I need time."

"Once the Grand Jury reaches a decision, it's too late to make an offer. Tell me something useful. Or tell Morell."

"What if my former employers don't want me to talk?"

"So you do have employers?"

Shit.

"You've been threatened?" Like he's asking about my paper cut.

"I'm saying what if."

"If you tell us who threatened you, we know who you work for." Anslinger slips into his camel hair coat. "And since you told us that, it means you're cooperating. We'll want to protect you."

"You got a card?"

"No."

The pony box counts beeps and booth number four goes dark. My heart slows down, my hands cease their cricket twitching. I can't leave, yet.

I drop another token into the box and the Glass Stripper is back, a blow-up sex doll, carnival prize dancing as though the window never opened. Had Anslinger shot me through the face, she'd dance for my bleeding corpse just the same. I slip her the money and she presses her palm against the glass like she's visiting me in prison. She holds her splayed fingers against the window while the numbers tick down. I press my palm in return to her jailhouse greeting and swallow the burning in my throat. It's when I know she sees me I want her the most. The lights go out.

The Glass Stripper waves, tickling the air with her fingertips. The slow guillotine descent of the window ends with a bindle in the tip slot. She remembers me.

Please don't be mad at me, Desiree.

ten

THE DIFFERENCE BETWEEN THE MAN ON PAROLE AND THE MAN ON DEATH ROW is sometimes two inches of locked bathroom door or a single moment's hesitation. The difference between those men and a chimpanzee is two percent of their genes and the difference between a man's healthy tissue and his tumor is even less. Every man and every insect are made from the same six molecules of DNA, the same five atoms. One of these atoms makes the difference between speed and cold medicine, between paint thinner and TNT. Every identical act is distinguished by its intent and every intent is judged by its action. The difference between consent and rape can be a single drink or a single word.

Everything in the universe is everything else. A man is a killer is a saint is a monkey is a cockroach is a goldfish is a whale, and the Devil is just the angel who asked for More.

Doomed but destined to forever want the closest thing beyond our grasp, we fled the trees, stood on our hind legs and reached with our new hands. We learned to sharpen sticks, then rocks, to scream, then grunt, then speak. We were hardwired for desire, and our wanting drove us to evolve, so we evolved wanting. More food, more fire and more off-spring. More gods. Gods for harvest, fire and fertility. One day, one god said, No more. No more other gods, no more of More. A million years of More were flushed away, cesspooling nine circles below the earth, a million years too late. Man's nature has been set to be unsatisfied.

Everyone craves the same grand version of every fortune-teller's surefire, shotgun guess list—money or love, and there's never enough. The richest men in the world scheme to become richer. Anyone serving time in a beige office cubicle knows this. Anyone paying mortgage on a beige house, spending what they don't have at beige strip malls on amusements for their beige children with beige futures, knows this. Every drink, roll of the dice or second glance at a woman whispers More into a man's ear when he's not listening to that one god, when he's looking where, or thinking what, he should not.

I've spent my life giving people their More. I'm a chemist.

A woman carries a torch for a lost love and her husband never knows. A man loses a child, a wife or a brother. Maybe it's his fault or maybe it isn't. People carry losses their whole lives, loss of a job, a friendship, a marriage, a reputation, a fortune or the life of a loved one. Some have regrets they feel every waking second, and some they feel in their sleep.

Imagine the one god himself has reversed his clock and reversed your regrets. Imagine knowing the bone-deep truth that whatever impossibility would make you truly happy has been granted. Imagine knowing you can once again hold your lost lover or your newborn child. Imagine what you feel during those first seconds of knowing. Now, imagine those first seconds last for days on end.

If you could buy that seventy-two-hour moment for the price of a tank of gas, would you? Go on, give it a try. God said it was okay.

Like I said, I'm a chemist. It's all coming back to me.

eleven

THE RIDGE OF YOUR SPINE BRUSHES THE TIP OF MY NOSE, THE SKIN SLOPING
from your shoulder blades grazes my lips, but my arms pass through a
hole in the air when I try to wrap them around you. My heart collapses
under its own sudden weight and falls into the bottomless black well of
my chest. I hold still and feel you again, a warm surge from that bottomless well sets my heart right and you're once more here beside me.

The blanket fell from my window and now streetlights shine from
the mirror. Room 621 glows like the surface of the moon. Another
room replaces mine when I close my eyes. Open, close, open, close.
One room swaps places with another, my field of vision changes like
flipping channels. I'm in your bedroom.

I met you, and now I'm standing in your room, the memories
spliced together with the connecting events nowhere to be found. I met
you, was abducted by aliens or brainwashed by the CIA, and now I'm
standing in your room. That missing stretch of time is in a syringe or
on microfilm, trapped in a bell jar within an underground vault
guarded by motion sensors and electric fences, but it's not in my head.

My reflection meets my fingertip with his own, Michelangelo's God
and Adam. The mirror bows like a sheet of taut plastic. I trace figure
eights and random glyphs in the glass and my finger leaves a warped
trail in its wake, like I'm six years old and playing with a puddle of pan-
cake syrup. The miniature Red Sea converges, each new stickman,

teepee or rocket ship fills in and fades in slow succession. We press palms, my reflection and I distorting each other from opposite sides of the liquid mirror. I'm flying on something, more acid of my own design. I've become better and bolder during that hole of haze I've leapfrogged between doses from the Glass Stripper.

My reflection says, "She still out there?" I hadn't seen his lips move in the twisting of the mirror, so I can't be certain.

"I need to lay low in here." My reflection didn't say anything, but Otto did. Blond, wearing jeans, a rugby shirt and glasses as thick as aquarium glass, he sat on a pillow in the corner. He's staring at his fingers and moving his hands slowly in front of his face, but once he starts talking, he doesn't stop.

"Chick's scary," he says. "The short-haired brunette friend of Desiree's out there. Hooked up with her and she got space freaky. Cuffed me with these chains held together with a chunk of ice. I'm thinking, 'Cool, I'll go with this,' and everything's great until she jams a finger up my ass, which I'm absolutely not cool with but I can't do shit. I want to stop her but, let me tell you, Finnish street names make terrible safe words. Pills she gave me, I couldn't feel my lips, much less form consonants. And she's been matching me two for one, so she drops out cold and I'm stuck for two and a half hours waiting for the ice to melt so I can get loose. Finally, I'm rolling her wheezing, naked body off my jeans and looking for my wallet, I see she's broken a goddamned nail off her examination finger. I'm freaked, like I want to run but don't want to slice myself up on the inside. Three days of yogurt, prunes and death threats screamed onto my answering machine. We haven't been properly introduced. I'm Otto."

"I know who you are."

"And you're Eric." He stands and offers his hand. I think he's reaching through the glass. I'm startled at first, but he's standing to one side of the mirror, beside my reflection. We shake hands, his flesh and bone.

He smacked the mirror with his middle finger. The surface quivered like a rubber sheet, our reflections bursting into moonlit confetti.

"Watch this." Otto pounded his fist against the wall. Concentric ripples spread across the pictures, window frame and the other walls. They undulated like the surface of a water bed, lapping at the corners.

"Eric?" The walls righted themselves, snapshot frozen, the instant you opened the door. "What was that?"

You're a silhouette in the doorway, but I can see your eyes in spite of the light flooding mine.

"Just talking to Otto," I said.

"Come outside, you should meet everyone."

"One second."

You blew me a kiss, then closed the door.

My heart beats faster at the sight of you, my blood sings at the sound of your voice and I don't want to move from this bed. I don't want to disturb your phantom skin against mine.

"This stuff is beautiful," Otto said. "Only God could have done better. Is there something I should know about you?"

"You know too much."

"Relax. I've known Desiree since I was a pup. She's been my best friend since she saved me from three brothers, five sisters and no father."

"Sad story."

"But typical."

"And you're clean?"

"You mean tapeworms? I'm clean. Desiree sees to that." Otto dropped his pants and hiked up his shirt. He did not ask me to return the courtesy.

"What does that mean?" I asked.

"Just what I said."

"What's your relationship with her?"

"You and I have business, buddy. Piles of cash with our names on it." He buckled his belt. "Quit sniffing my ass and speak English."

"Are you now, or have you ever been, sexually involved with Desiree?"

"No. Not even close. She's got nice legs, I'll give her that. But she's not my type. She takes care of me and I look after her. I'm protective, that way. If you want her, make your move, but you'd be wise to ditch the jealousy. It'll cloud your thinking. Besides, she doesn't know you made this stuff, and you're never going to tell her." He tapped the mirror, sending silver ripples through the glass.

"This is good," he said.

"You see what I see?"

"Yes. What do you call it?"

"What do you mean?"

"Mad Hatter," said Otto.

"I'm not following you."

"The best batch in the world won't go anywhere without a good name. If you're ever at a loss, you can't go wrong with a reference to Alice."

"Thanks for the advice."

"Can you do it again?"

"These were an experiment. I was trying something different."

"A fortunate mistake. Can you do it again?"

"Of course. I'm just not set up for it. What little gear I've got has miles of wear on it, and the rest is hacked together from scrap."

I was using athletic water bottles for sep funnels. Junk stores and yard sales had yielded three vintage chemistry sets from which I'd salvaged lab-grade glass. They don't make those anymore, because of guys like me.

"Let me show you something." Otto took a candle from the dresser.

There were four or five of them, and none had ever been lit. Its under-side had been hollowed out. He removed a roll of bills as thick as his own wrist.

"I can set you up," he said. "Get you all the gear you want, get you safe and isolated."

"Put that back," I said.

"It's not hers. It's mine."

"She holds your money for you?"

He said nothing, tossing the fat roll up and down.

"She doesn't know it's here?" I said.

"No, she doesn't. That's not all of it. I spread it around."

"You're safe until she lights that candle."

"She won't. Listen," he pressed the roll of bills into my hand, "I can unload whatever else you've got for three times what you're selling it for, five or six times what it cost you to make it. I can make it worth your while."

"I should get out there."

I don't remember the occasion, much less the names and faces of everyone present. I do remember your friends coasting on the acid they knew I'd brought but didn't know I'd made.

They sought me out until I took refuge in your room, and did the same when I returned to the group. *Where did you get this? Can you get more?*

Along with the hand-holding circles, face touching, rambling on about the beauty of the universe and the presence of God in all things, they had a Darwinian appreciation for me and my contribution. As my stature rose within the group, so did your proximity to me, from touching my shoulder during conversation, to leaning at my side or sit-ting on my lap, to holding my hand as you said your good-byes at the end of the night after the Mad Hatters had burned off in a clean, thirty-minute comedown.

"Are you staying?" You pressed your nose into my neck.

"I'm going to run out for a bit," I said, and you wrapped your arms around me. "I'll be right back, I'm just getting some wine." Your hold grew tighter. You said no.

"I promise, just give me a minute."

"How long?"

"Half an hour."

"Take Otto with you. For collateral."

"Is he staying too?"

"Don't be ridiculous."

You kissed me. For the length of the kiss, the Mad Hatters came back.

"If you follow the news," Otto rode shotgun, talking in an auctioneer's blue streak, "busts are almost always in the inner cities. If you trust the numbers about the drug economy, and believe that it's purely an inner-city problem, then the streets of ghettos and barrios would be swamped with dealers, and the buyers would queue up like an East German bread line.

"The major shit moves through here," he said. He'd guided me into suburbia. Skin-colored houses with white pickups and boats in their driveways. "And I mean major."

He reached into the backseat and heaved a black duffle the size of a small tree stump into his lap. Beneath two layers of waterproof canvas and nylon lay an ingot of bills. They were sheathed in plastic, the top layer all Jacksons.

"This time, it isn't mine. I'm a way station."

"Zip that up." My eyes went to the rearview mirror out of instinct. Every pair of headlights was cause for alarm. "Now."

"All twenties. Nonsequential and unmarked. I've checked 'em, I know." He closed the inner and outer bags and said, "this thing weighs thirty-five pounds. You want to know how much this totals?"

"No."

"Whatever. You're the only other person I've told about it. I gotta deliver it tonight and they're going to count it, every last bill. You'll find out."

"I'll wait outside."

"Relax. You'll like these people."

We made two stops, maybe three. Some details are sharper than others, and they all run together. The houses were the same, I remember, white walls, white carpets, and children's art projects on the refrigerators. Each visit, someone offered us a light beer and a seat on the couch in front of a wide-screen television where I waited while Otto exchanged one bag for another.

Otto's people drove minivans with baby seats, their floors littered with fast-food wrappers, school newsletters and sports equipment. They owned boats and jet skis, campers and trucks with bumper stickers broadcasting their political party or proclaiming their children's honor-student status. They wore Little League coaching windbreakers and T-shirts branded with water-ski equipment dealers or lake resorts. They had gold credit cards, frequent-flyer miles, golf clubs, satellite dishes, video games, swimming pools and dirt bikes.

They told sad stories, stories about playing football in high school or sexual conquests in college, about the concerts they'd seen and how much they drank, about the long hair or the earring they once had. They told stories about the muscle car they had as a teenager, about the band they played in or the bike they used to race.

The details are as blurry as they are dull. What remains vivid above all else is the size of the duffle bags Otto was moving, the bets he placed on games during the stops, and our handshake agreement on the drive back. We were in business.

You were staring at the moon from your front yard when the lights from my Galaxie flared against your hair like a torch.

"That was more than half an hour." You grabbed my belt buckle and pulled me into you. "I wasn't sure you were coming back."

"I thought you were a fortune-teller."

"People tell their fortunes for me. I just listen, give them a few details and they fill in the blank spots. They think it's all me, but it's not. They believe what they want to."

"You must be good if you make a living at it."

You took my hands, laced your fingers with mine and pulled them behind your back, locking us together. The tip of your nose brushed my face and it felt cold, so I kissed it.

"You kissed my nose."

"It was cold."

"Are you trying to seduce me?"

"You'll know."

"Will I, now?"

"Yes. All of your willpower will dissolve when I decide to seduce you." I kept a straight face for as long as I could, but you started laughing.

I pulled away but you took my bottom lip in your teeth and held me there. You let go after a moment, looking over my shoulder to the Galaxie where Otto lingered.

"Otto, stay," you said, then kissed me again. "You too. Don't worry, he's on the couch."

I remember my hand on the sweat-slick small of your back, your wet leg slung over mine and "hold still" hot-whispered into my ear and I did but you couldn't and you moaned my name, lost in the teeth marks you left on my chest. I drank dark wine pooled in the cleft of your back and licked every inch of you, then held you until your breathing told me you were asleep, but you never let go of me.

twelve

THE TYRANNOSAURUS HAD COLLAPSED INTO A MANGLED HEAP, ITS LEGS BLOWN from beneath it after decades of drunken target practice. Its bullet-pocked body lay in a pile of broken concrete amid spent shell casings, bottle shards, hubcaps and sagebrush, the exposed rebar skeleton baking under the desert sun. Otto emptied his bladder into the monster's dead, frozen jaw.

"Whaddaya think used to be here?"

He shifted his stance to coat the face and neck while he spoke. The smell stung my nostrils and I moved upwind. Fifty feet from Otto, an empty swimming pool lay in front of a row of abandoned motel rooms.

"A gas station," I said.

"That looks like a swimming pool." Otto zipped up and walked to the concrete cavity half filled with tumbleweeds.

"Swimming pools have water in them."

"Definitely a pool," he said, surveying from the edge with the gravity of a plane crash investigator. "This was a motel of some kind."

"I envy your keen sense of the obvious, Otto."

"Dinosaurs ate all of the tourists, before target practice from the locals drove them to extinction." He unzipped his pants again, and pissed into the layer of mud below. "Then for a while it was a tumbleweed brothel."

"What are you doing?"

"Marking my territory."

We'd been on the road for over three hours, enduring the Mojave heat. The Galaxie had been painted with eight coats of factory crimson and loaded with four new whitewalls. With less than 8,000 miles on a rebuilt engine, it was in perfect working order, except for the air-conditioning. I'd brought a bag full of bottled water, sunblock and spare T-shirts, and had sweat through four of them.

Signs throughout the desert had warned of the dangers of flash floods and hitchhikers. A truck tire had been submerged halfway into the dirt where we'd parked, then painted white, with BUS STOP in red letters. The road stretched to the horizon in both directions with nobody coming from either. Anyone expecting a bus would die waiting.

"I don't like being late," I said, checking my watch.

"Breathe, buddy." Otto zipped up again. "We're less than four miles away. Let's toss the Frisbee."

"We're four miles away but you couldn't wait. Jesus. I don't want to toss anything, I want to move. Are you finished?"

"Maybe. I want to sniff around for a minute."

"There's a chance you might find an actual toilet," I said. "I'm going to make a call."

"From where?"

A gas station stood adjacent to the motel, the parking lot more potholes than asphalt. One of four pumps lay on its side, ripped from the ground by a drunken dinosaur hunter behind the wheel of a pickup. Nobody had removed the GAS COLD SODAS ICE sign at the edge of the highway though someone had boarded up the windows and spray-painted FOR SALE across the plywood. The phone booth, however, was pristine, with the receiver on the hook and not so much as a crack in the glass, as though it had been installed that morning.

"There's a phone," I said. "Over there."

"It's abandoned."

"I'm not getting an oil change. Wave when you're done sniffing."

Otto started toward the dilapidated motel rooms and shouted, "Watch for dinosaurs."

I slid the door shut and sealed out the midday silence of the desert. I heard my blood rushing through my ears, then the hum of the wires, the sleepy rasp of your voice.

"Did I wake you?"

"It's okay. I was just napping. How did your interview go?"

"It's in about half an hour. I'm not worried. How's business on the promenade?"

"Slow night downtown. What's the position you're interviewing for?"

"Short-term consulting. Lab stuff I don't want to bore you with."

"No, it's fascinating. You can tell me."

Christ, leave it alone.

"I don't know the exact nature of the contract. Are you working later?"

"No, I was hoping to see you. Are you coming back?"

Maybe. I didn't know where I was going, with whom I was meeting, whether I'd make my next call from jail or the return trip in my own trunk. Throughout the drive, the scenarios ran through my brain in ceaseless succession. Otto was a cop. An informant. He worked for a rival chemist. I should confront him. I should abandon him. Each notion negated by its own idiocy the instant it surfaced.

"There's a chance I'll need to meet someone else tomorrow," I said. "I'll find a hotel and crash for the night, then drive back tomorrow afternoon."

"No." Your plea melted me. "Come over tonight and you can drive back tomorrow morning."

"You want me to double back to Riverside twice in two days?"

"I want to see you."

"I want to see you too. I'll be back as soon as I can."

"Please. I won't keep you up late, I promise."

The feeling of being so wanted was new to me.

"I'll do what I can. I should go now."

"Hey," you said. "What color are my eyes?"

"Come on. Don't do that."

In that second, the wire stretching from the desert to your bed became infinite, and every word was a ripple in the middle of the ocean that became a crashing wave thousands of miles away. I spoke too quickly and I could hear my resentment crash down on you from a distance.

"I'm sorry," you said. "I miss you. I'll see you whenever you get back, okay?"

"Your eyes are green."

"Good guess."

I could hear you smile through the wires.

"Bluish green."

"You're sounding like a palm reader."

I'd taken a photograph from your refrigerator and dropped it into my bag before I'd left, a snapshot of you laughing somewhere warm and sunny with an umbrella drink in your hand, but I didn't need it. Just as it did when I spoke to you that day from the phone, your face comes into focus more and more as I hold you here beside me.

"There's a large speck in the blue green of your right eye. A small bump on the bridge of your nose. A lock of your hair always falls over one eye, and you've got a tiny mole on your right cheek, right on the corner of your smile."

"You have quite a memory."

"My memory's terrible," I said. "But I can picture you when I hear your voice."

"I'll help you with your memory."

"Fill in the blank spots?"

"Yeah. That's what I'm good at."

"So long as I can see you."

"In your mind or in person?"

"Both."

You sighed, and the waves going over the wire washed me with calm.

"I miss you." You broke the silence. "Please come back tonight, if you can."

"I'll try. I miss you too."

We said our good-byes. I listened to the electric monotone of the dead line for a minute before I hung up. I opened the glass floodgates and the miles of silence crashed through.

The house had been trashed, abandoned, boarded up, squatted in, sold, reoccupied, raided, reabandoned and reboarded. Otto and I waited on the porch, four miles up the road from the ghost motel. The sky looked bigger, a stretch of luminous blue with clouds so massive I didn't know how they stayed in the air.

"It's sturdy," Otto said, like a child telling himself there's nothing under the bed or in the closet. "You'll know when someone's coming and they won't be able to get in easily."

"If the Feds are coming, it doesn't matter how sturdy it is," I said.

"I'm not talking about the Feds. I'm talking about people who are pissed and looking for you. I'm talking about home invasions and pay-back."

"Otto, who are we working for?"

Somebody named Hoyle ran everything. The supply chain, the distribution chain and everyone involved. Hoyle's word was final. Hoyle didn't want acid. Acid didn't make people want more acid. Hoyle wanted the things that woke up the slumbering instinct for More, and woke it with a vengeance. Otto had never met Hoyle. He knew someone who had, and for whom we were waiting.

A wake of desert dirt billowed from the tires of a white van. I know that van, though I've never seen it before. My memory's stuck in a loop because I'm remembering things that haven't happened yet, the order of events from yesterday and the day before collapse into the events prior to the fire. Here and now collide with then and there and, for a second, Manhattan White and Toe Tag are standing in my room at the Firebird with flames engulfing everything while I lie with my arms around you in the middle of nowhere. The moment passes, each note of memory arranging itself from noise to symphony.

Manhattan White approached on foot. Otto made himself scarce. White's son sat on the open back end of the van, ice-cream stains on his shirt and snot running from his nose. He played with a pair of wire clippers.

"My name's White."

We've met.

"I'm Eric."

"I know."

"You got a first name?"

"They call me Manhattan. White will do. I understand you're a chemist, Eric."

"I am."

"What I want to know is, why?"

"Can you be a little clearer?"

"Why did I drive all this way to meet you? Why should our business back you when I've got a hundred guys who can do the same thing? Why is it you're better than they are?"

"I don't know who they are, White, so I don't know if I'm better."

"I hear you've opened a window to God."

"That was an experiment."

"Is that what you want to do?"

"What I want to do is something nobody else has done."

"Again, my question is, why?"

"Couldn't tell you. Maybe some unresolved questions about God from when I was younger. All I know is I've got the focus and the patience for it and there's not many other jobs that will indulge me that way."

"We're not here to indulge you, either, or help you with your childhood issues. We're here to make a profit and to do so inconspicuously. You're here to build us a lab, for which you will be well paid."

"So you say. Let's have a look."

White unlocked three deadbolts on the front door. The inside looked as though a family of shut-ins had survived a decade of collective agoraphobia on canned beer, frozen dinners, cigarettes and television, and were finally evicted by a tribe of drunk monkeys driving snowblowers.

"What's that noise?" I asked. I couldn't tell where it was coming from at first, but it sounded like a finger squeaking across a wet windowpane, thousands of them.

"What noise?"

"Is there an attic here?"

White looked to the ceiling. "Of course," he said. "Bats. Don't worry. They're harmless."

"And dirty."

White pressed the solitude and space the house afforded. I countered with the need to disconnect the gas for the heating and stove because I couldn't have open flames. I wanted to map the circuits so I could shut down certain outlets and work with the select few I needed.

"That sounds excessive," White said.

"How many accidents have you had to cover up?" I asked.

"A few. It's a numbers game and accidents are part of the risk."

"It's only a numbers game when you leave it to amateurs or chance," I said, then pointed to the outlets at floor level. "See those?"

"Yeah, they're plugs. And?"

"And they're not grounded, so if you're pulling too much current from them, they tend to spark. That's why you've got those burn marks on the slots. You can have either fumes or sparks, but you can't have both."

"You want to rewire the place and ground the power. Not cheap."

"For starters. Lesson two: ether. We'll be using it in quantity. It's colorless, odorless and inflammable."

"What's the problem?"

"Not unflammable, inflammable, so the fumes can, and will, blow."

"I hear you, Eric. Jesus, fix the sparks, then."

"It doesn't need sparks. Ether is heavier than air, so the vapors flow to ground level and then build up. Most lab fires happen when the fumes reach a wall socket and spontaneously ignite. You know the rest."

Time and materials were needed to prep the place, all of which were alien to White, but my list of gear was old news because he and his organization were in the business of procuring them for their legions of pyromaniac amateurs.

"We got guys everywhere working for us, and our guys have guys working for them. Most of them are runners," White began.

Runners, or coyotes, who worked at piecemealing together large stashes of matchbooks, road flares and cold medicine to avoid the Man's eyes. One of Hoyle's runners, so far down the chain nobody knew his name, used a counterfeit license, provided by the chain, for making certain purchases. He also used it to gain entry into a nightclub where he got hammered on some sugary girl drink, made the wrong move on the wrong woman and wouldn't take no for an answer until he heard it from the doorman's flashlight. The cops pulled him over later on a suspected DUI. They seized two gallons of hospital-grade iodine in his trunk. Coyote sobered up in County with eight gang-bangers tattooed like a collective flesh-and-blood Sistine Chapel. He didn't shower for four days pending arraignment and refused to call anyone.

He cut a deal and the DA cut him loose with a tapeworm stuck to his ribs.

"Get the bag, son," White shouted over to his van.

The boy hopped out, dragging with him a large, plastic bundle. The drooling man-boy moved with an odd grace, shifting his weight and anchoring his feet, hauling the bag from the van. It struck the dirt with a noise like a coconut wrapped in a wet towel. As much as I didn't want to look, I knew better than to look away.

"My son does all of this," said White. "Drains all of their fluids out and wraps them up. This happens if you fail a performance review and we fire you, like when this kid got scared and decided he could wear a tapeworm to a drop."

The head looked mummified, wrapped in cheesecloth or surgical gauze with stains seeping through in different stages of yellow, red and brown. The body was wrapped in a single layer of chicken wire.

"We'll dump him when we're done here. Toe Tag weighed his stomach down with rocks so he'll sink. The bottom feeders get through the chicken wire and pick the flesh from the bone. There's catfish the size of dogs in some of the these lakes out here. You don't want to order fish at any of the mom-and-pop joints between here and New Mexico."

thirteen

I'D SAY THE BUGS ARE MOCKING ME BUT THEY'RE NOT PROGRAMMED FOR THAT. The fuzzy logic of mockery doesn't justify the engineering cost. Instead, they record everything with heat-sensitive cameras and motion-triggered microphones. They're programmed to eat wallpaper paste, grease stains and bread crumbs, to shit into carpet, drop eggs into baseboard cracks, and they're built for speed. I've only caught a few.

The autopsy project has taken on a life of its own as I take the lives of more bugs. Specimens lie splayed onto cardboard dug from the trash, stripped and pinned with paperclips and thumbtacks. I've checked antennae polarity between every possible configuration, without a spark, an arc or a hint of current.

These weren't built with silicon circuits. All the foil in the world won't stop these bleeding-edge, bioengineered organisms because they're bred, not built, for transferring data the same way they've done for millions of years through dances, wing-flutter code and antenna semaphores. They spread news of food, danger, a new nesting location, my running solitaire statistics and bathroom habits.

Their engineering evolves with each generation, the progeny faster and their camouflage better. They hide in the fluttering shadows thrown by swaying power lines outside my window, or the shimmering reflections from a glass of water. They can look like patterns in the hallway carpet, red diamonds with yellow highlights, black squares like processor chips or irregular blobs from coffee stains or blood. Snap on a light and instead of scattering, they freeze where they're crawling and disappear.

They move in the dark, legions of them on every surface of my room and my skin. Sometimes I'll think I've stepped on a slippery pebble before the exoshell cracks like an apple skin and there's something wet beneath my foot, something else scurrying over my toes. They whisper to each other, monitor my sleep, fluid intake, pulse, temperature and record my conversations. The ones I've killed by accident or design are bigger than the rest, relay points or data backups, so they're easier to catch. Their system is rife with redundancies, so the death of one messenger doesn't derail the flow of data. My recent specimens flutter inside an empty baby food jar, awaiting the cockroach chop shop. They climb atop one another, scrambling for the punctured lid and fall backward like marbles rattling against the glass. The noise keeps me awake.

I pull the sheets from my bed, tie the corners together and throw the bundle out the window. I tear open a box of Borax, dumping it into every corner and crevice I find. Someone knocks and I have a small heart attack.

I answer the door in my underwear, my body dusted with boric acid.

"Have you been talking?" Suit and tie. He looks familiar.

"I've been cleaning."

"You were supposed to call me with an address."

"Are you an exterminator?

"I'm your lawyer." He steps into my room without invitation. "We have business," he says. "While you're housecleaning, Anslinger is burying you. He doesn't sleep and he doesn't stop working. He's a machine. Do you understand me?"

My memory comes into focus. Morell.

"Can I get you anything?" I ask. "Water? I have a sink."

Decades of junkie sex and contract hits have stained the mattress with dark Rorschach shapes. One looks like a dog, another a clown. Morell sits on the bare corner beside a burning nun, his briefcase in his lap.

"What have you been using?" he asks.

"Boric acid."

"No, you. What have you been shooting?"

"Nothing. I'm clean and I can prove it if you've got a coffee cup."

"No, you are not clean. And I can't help you unless you are."

I thrust my arms out, wrists up, dotted with the cigarette burns. My bites aren't as advanced as those on Jack and the Beanstalk. They must be scratching too much.

"Insects. They're eating me in my sleep. The place is crawling with them," I explain, and at night they're everywhere. Most of them are too fast for me. I slap at the night table corners and shadow specks on my bedspread, but they're gone before my palm hits. I thought they were planting tracking chips, but they're not mechanical. They're marking me, like cats pissing on furniture, so the squads assigned to a different detail don't monitor the wrong target.

"Let's move you somewhere else," says Morell.

"They'll follow me. Or signal others. I think they work for Anslinger."

"I'm going to assume you haven't recalled anything helpful." Morell sighs, staring at the cockroach chop shop. "Here's my card. Again." He stands, reaching into his pocket. "Check in with me in two days, whether you remember anything or not. And if you do consider moving, let me know this time." He leaves.

"They can still track me," I say to his back.

The drones in my head explode into a furious, flapping cloud. This must be what a brainstorm feels like. Like missing the first bug hidden in plain sight, I had been looking everywhere except under my nose. A stretch of bites covers both forearms, a finger's width from a vein. Big, small, small. Small. The different-sized bugs make the different-sized bites, unless I've picked or scratched and inflamed one of them, which destroys the sequence. Small, small, small. Small, small. Small, big, small. Small. Small. If they can track me, I can track them.

They could be sex toys or time machines as much as pipes, lined up on shelves labeled "Not for Sale to Persons Under 18 Years of Age" like rows of sleeping, mutant genies below a mural of Jimi Hendrix. Smaller pipes, along with scales, mirrors and scores of paraphernalia are spread beneath glass cases like alien medical instruments.

A display of makeup sits atop a jewelry case. I grab a bottle of nail polish the luminous yellow of a school crossing sign. I hand it to the white kid with dreadlocks behind the register and ask for a black lightbulb.

I can tell my room is different. Everything is shifted so slightly.

fourteen

THEY PREACHED ARMAGEDDON, THE COMING RACE WAR, THE OVERTHROW OF our Zionist-occupied government and they stank. I see balls of fog in lieu of faces, like my jail-cell mirror reflection. They were target practicing in their living room with a pellet gun. The row of shredded and tattered stuffed animals is on my right, then my left, and the walls change color as one time and place bleeds into the next, the details slipping from beneath my memory like mercury.

You stroke my wrist, back and forth, the way you did when you couldn't sleep, so you wouldn't let me, either.

Their nicknames fit them too well or not at all. Pinstripe, Gash, Flash, Joker. They sounded like dwarfs, or candy bars. Ashtrays, cheeseburger wrappers, razorblades and hamster pipes on the coffee table, scorched foil and dried blood in the bathroom sink. A mound of underwear below the empty cardboard spool soaked up the toilet overflow. Iodine stains on the ceiling, the stench of brake fluid and road flares, the burn marks outnumbered only by their excuses for the damage. Silence drooled from their open mouths when I asked them the molecular weight of carbon, the vapor pressure of toluene or the flashpoint of diethyl ether.

The Chain was going about it all wrong, I'd told White, trusting amateurs scattered among unconnected labs. Amateur cooks don't-follow formulas as they should. They don't master the basics and think they can improvise. They create emergencies, which create problems for everyone.

"You will work in teams of two," I explained. "One team will tear strikers from the matchbooks—"

"Can we use matchboxes?" one of them asked, cutting me off.

"Yes. You can use matchboxes. Two of you will tear strikers from the books."

"Or the boxes."

"Or the boxes," I paused, waiting for the next interruption, which never came. "And two of you will sand the strikers with a Dremmel."

"What's a Dremmel?"

"Don't mind him, he's new," another one said.

"You're all new."

"Nuh uh. I've been doing this shit for years."

"Not my way, you haven't."

"You need to relax, man. I can handle this."

I hadn't driven that distance to take shit from some toothless tractor-pulling tweaker.

"Explain that." I pointed to the scorch mark on the coffee table.

"It was an accident."

"And that?" The rust-colored fog stained into their ceiling was from evaporated iodine. "How many accidents have you had?" I kicked a glass bowl, already cracked from sloppy handling and coated with the residue amateur cooks leave for cops to scrape up. That seemed to end it.

"This is a Dremmel." I held up the cordless drill, fitted with a sanding bit. "Do a five count," I said. "Five strokes, all the same direction.

Not too quickly, but not too hard. You don't want the strikers getting too hot, and you do not want to drop them, whatever you do." I demonstrated the slow, gentle strokes for removing the dust from the matchbook striker.

This crew was going to harvest phosphorus. Other crews would do likewise, others would purify iodine or harvest another precursor. Each lab would specialize in a single ingredient, producing far more of an individual precursor than their previous yields of finished product with fewer procedures so a reduced risk of an accident. Labs would be linked by coyotes who transferred cash, materials or finished chemicals between specific points. Each pair of runners would have their own set of codes and signals. None of the crews would know who or where the other crews were. Anyone caught had nobody to roll over on. If anyone went missing or was more than five minutes late, the crew was to cut and run.

"We keep your crews," I'd told White. "None of that changes. We split the duties. We assign each crew a specific job. The same group can produce at least twice as much precursor as they can product."

"And the product?" White asked. "What about it?"

Everything converged at the first house Otto and I had set up, Oz, where we'd take care of the final manufacturing. Hoyle got his More, but with less money and less risk. I got paid, got White off my back, and had more time to work on my own.

"We do the final synthesis at Oz," I said. "In the meantime, the guys you have in place are doing fewer operations with fewer solvents and less equipment. There's less risk, and in the event of an accident, less damage to product and gear, less likelihood of detection and less to disperse in an emergency."

The monotony posed the biggest threat. Guys like these took their payment in product, so they did things like sort garbage bags full of hole-punch confetti according to color when they weren't working. They'd fixate on details, like sanding off matchbook strikers. They'd lose sight of the bigger picture, like the growing pile of dust and the errant sparks. The flash hit someone's face or lit their hair on fire. They tripped over a bucket of acetone. One thing leads to another, another being the lab in flames.

The collected dust looked like anthills made from red dirt and glitter and was so fine it stained your fingernails. If you didn't wear a mask, you'd sneeze blood.

"No more than a quarter ounce at a time should pile up," I said.

"How much is that?"

"Twice as much as you have here." I indicated the reddish brown pile built up on the worktable.

"How can you be sure?"

"You got a scale?" My patience was gone.

"You took our gear," he said.

He was right, I had. Starting from scratch, my way or no way at all, with White's backing.

The pause gave the impulse whisper an opening, and I struck a match. The pile flared into a plume of sparks and rotten smoke. The four of them recoiled like cavemen before their first thunderstorm. The flames die down within seconds. I normally wouldn't be so reckless, but I had to make an impression.

"Too much piles up," I said, "and you're risking a fire. A spark from the Dremmel or dropping a hot striker is all it takes. You guys have nearly burned this place down a dozen times, but you still cowered like a bunch of schoolgirls. That happens, you knock something over or catch yourself on fire, whatever, everything goes up in flames."

"You still took our scale. How are we supposed to know when we're done?" With that, he left the room. He'd thrown the last word and left me hanging. I couldn't afford doubts from the rest of them.

"You guys want out?" I surveyed their faces, mute and slack from the fire. "Say the word. No skin off my back. I pay you now, you walk and you stay walked. Or, you do it my way and stay for the long haul."

For effect, I pulled out the fat roll I'd been saving for Otto. He was too eager to hit the tables, sometimes.

"We're cool," said the new guy. The other two nodded.

Which name went to which face, I don't know, except Pinstripe, who was either nineteen and drug weathered, or thirty-five and hormone deficient. He had beard stubble but his teeth were small and spaced apart, like he'd never lost his first set. He had the wide eyes and button nose of an infant with the overgrown ears of an old man. His face is more vivid than the rest because he was screaming while I dumped baking soda onto his shivering naked body to stop the muriatic acid from burning him any further. His top layer of skin fell away in wet strips, the skin beneath it showing red and slippery like an oiled sunburn. Clumps of hair had melted together around one of his ears, which had swollen into a knot of blistered cartilage.

"I was going to give it to you for your trunk." He was sobbing as he spoke, trying to snow me with some cheap excuse like some eight-year-old while spitting out a stream of expletives with "hospital" thrown in every three or four words. Two jugs of acid lay on their sides, the bedroom carpet beneath them melted into lumpy plastic. He'd been out of my sight for more than an hour since he stormed out of my earlier session. The spill made no sense. There was no sign that he'd been cooking on his own or trying to hide materials from me, which meant it was the kind of senseless accident that happened regularly with White's hand-picked crews.

"Hospital means jail, which means prison." I said this to the others, then to Pinstripe, "you'll get help but you'll get it my way. New guy, tell me you've got something for him."

"What something?"

"Something for his pain."

"Yeah, we got something."

"Get it. Now."

After Pinstripe chased three Valium with a quart of warm beer, he lay shivering like a prison quarantine victim, covered in white powder like he'd been treated for lice.

"Just sit there. New guy, it starts to burn again, douse him with more baking soda." I took my keys from my pocket.

"Where you going?"

"Getting him help." Any medic in these parts would know what muriatic acid burns meant, since it was clear Pinstripe hadn't been cleaning pools or been near any water for some time.

"You can use our phone," said one of them. "We got one in the kitchen."

"Not anymore."

The highway off-ramp was a truck-stop oasis in the middle of nowhere, with two diners, two gas stations and four motels advertising the low room rates that indicated their proximity to a prison. I stopped at one of the diners, asked for a cup of coffee and a roll of quarters then called for White from a pay phone. The number I dialed wasn't for White, but the pager for the anonymous someone who paged him in turn. It changed monthly, as did the four-digit code to signal the callback. I waited for three minutes before the phone rang and White said, "Go."

"I've got a Wicker Man," I said.

"How bad?" White sounded amused, enjoying the prospect of pinning a misfire on me.

"Alive," I said. "And smokeless. That's the last of the good news. Otherwise, it's serious and he's screaming for a doctor."

"You had this under control."

"You hired the amateurs."

"Where are you?"

"The Lighthouse."

"I'll be there in three hours."

I hung up, knowing those were going to be his last words and that maybe I got the drop on him.

By the time I returned, Pinstripe had been doused with more baking soda and lay curled into a fetal ball from the cocktail of shock and Valium, his eyes closed and mouth open. The crew was hard at work, and ready to learn.

I didn't trust these clowns with heating solvents, so I opted for slower, room-temperature methods. We dumped the striker dust into sterilized glass jars filled with denatured alcohol, which had been prepared at another lab, and lined the jars of foggy, brown liquid on the kitchen counter. They were instructed to agitate them every five minutes for half an hour, then double filter the mixture and let the alcohol evaporate. Two extractions with two different solvents followed, yielding three ounces of pure, red phosphorus. These guys could produce four pounds each week if they did as they were told.

Before we'd finished, Pinstripe was in the front seat of White's van, Toe Tag in the back playing with a pair of naked, plastic action figures, his face stained with fruit punch and chocolate.

"You can take care of him?" I asked. White chewed on a cuticle. "Right?"

"Stupid question for such a smart guy," he answered.

"Remember that the next time you recruit a bunch of your son's classmates."

"Right. Here's the good news. Hoyle wants an increase in production."

"I am increasing production. That's why I'm out here."

"You're out here so you can give yourself more playtime with your chemistry set."

"Yes, and so I can toilet train this battalion of idiots you've got scattered between L.A. and Texas."

"Hoyle's looking for a quadruple increase in quota," White kept on, as though I hadn't said a thing and he were addressing a mass audience. "And he's looking to you."

"No," I said, White's bullshit stank more than he knew. "Hoyle's looking to triple. You upped it."

"I'm with you on this, Eric." White smiled. I'd nailed him, cold. "I'm taking care of problems, trying to free you up to do what you do best."

"The whole point of the setup I proposed was to cut me loose."

"You want to play mad scientist. In a facility, Eric, which we paid for."

"Which will earn itself back after thirty days, White. And yes, I want to be left alone. To work."

"And do what?"

"I'm not sure yet. That's why it's called experimenting."

White rolled his eyes. I counted to three. Raising my voice would alarm Toe Tag.

"You know anything about synthesizing new analogues of known alkaloids?" I asked. Once again, White took to grooming his nails with his teeth. "Or do you know—"

"Whatever you do in there," White cut me off, "we own." He buckled his seat belt.

"Tell Hoyle we'll triple production at a third of his current cost."

"You can promise me that? More importantly, can you promise

Hoyle that?"

"The production increase is a favorable estimate. The costs are certain." If he argued with me in this arena, he couldn't win. He knew that. "The only variables are whatever clowns you've given me to work with at the other sites. After today, I'd suggest you wait by your phone."

"Are you prepared to answer to Hoyle should the increase not occur?"

"The increase will occur. Give him that estimate, and as we'll very likely exceed it, we'll make him even happier. And if you're so skeptical, why did you give me a higher number?"

"I hope you're right."

"I am right. Do something about Pinstripe. I have work to do."

Hoyle wanted more of what made people want More. I didn't. Too much More and the customer shoots out the ass end of a twelve-day jag a pistol-waving, fly-swatting zombie. Someone in the distribution chain landed in a trauma center getting a screwdriver pulled out of their chest and the doctor filled out a report. Hoyle didn't care if someone got hurt; Hoyle cared when someone else asked questions. When that happened, Toe Tag put down his pudding cup and came out of his playroom.

A bone-deep craving is its own sales pitch. The club drugs couldn't compete with that, so I took my cues from the people who sold blue jeans, wristwatches and sneakers, the experts who convince everyone they need More when they don't. The experts had a formula, and I was good at formulas. The formula called for selling ideas before things, and the ideas were only as good as their labels. Otto had it right all along, the best batch in the world won't go anywhere without a good name.

Otto and I spent as much time with scratchpads as lab gear. We consulted music videos, soft drink commercials and fashion magazines. We brainstormed dye mixtures, stencil logos and shapes for pillpress molds.

Truckers were traditional. They wanted Black Beauties, Red Devils and Yellow Jackets. We added our own Johnnies and Ronnies, named after porn stars renowned for their stamina. We made Diesels, Choppers, Block Sixes, Straight Eights and Road Dogs whose mechanical names spoke of the job they did to the motorhead taking them.

What suburban white kids espoused as rebellion was, in truth, disposable income personified. We mass branded their counterculture symbols and sold them back in pill form. Abductors were popular, as were Strobes, Probes and Roswells. Trends changed by the week and we were scant minutes behind. Whether it's desert dispatch and chicken wire enforcement or a beige cubicle and a 401(k), it's the same game. Manufacturing, R&D, distribution, sales and marketing. I had the pins in the map before I ever met White.

People had to be dependable. If someone said they were going to be at a certain place at a certain time, they needed to be there. How late they were was directly proportional to how much time they needed to rendezvous in a public restroom or the back of a utility van and get wired with a tapeworm and briefed by the bug machines. If someone brought a friend, that someone was cut off, permanently.

White said tell me what you need and who uses it and we'll take care of you. White arrives at Oz in the heat of noon. I've sweat through my T-shirt and Otto was gone to Las Vegas again but that was fine with me because we'd made some improvements in the lab that I wanted kept quiet. We'd brought a floor safe out in a rented truck, and spent the morning hammering through the space in the foundation to drop it in. It wasn't for cash being transferred, it was for our own.

I saw White's van outside and could have sworn I heard more than one set of footsteps, but nobody said anything and I waited for the knock that never came. I stepped outside, wiping sweat from my forehead and White was waiting patiently, looking through a stack of documents.

"We've arranged for the documents for front companies," White says, "as well as putting the title to the house under an alias. My associate has taken care of the paperwork for us."

I hadn't noticed him, at first.

"No disrespect, Manhattan, but you need to tell me if you'll be bringing anyone else. I mean, somebody I haven't met."

He was standing out in front of the house, and he was about my age, a little younger, a little older, it was hard to say. Red hair and blue eyes, dressed in a dark gray oil jacket over a gray T-shirt of almost the same shade. Just over his jacket pocket, where a grease monkey might tuck his pen and tire gauge, was an oval of stitching where the embroidered name tag had been removed. He was wearing tan work pants and dark brown work boots, and with the combination of colors, dark grey and tan, sitting in the sharp daytime shadows of the dilapidated desert house, he was invisible. I didn't even see him out of the corner of my eye and he was completely still and expressionless. Except for his red hair, there was nothing distinct about him at all. It took me a moment to realize what was off about him, and it was the fact that, as natural-looking as his blue-collar wardrobe might have been, it was only slightly worn. Otherwise, his clothes were immaculately cleaned and pressed and he had only put them on moments ago after giving his boots a final spit polish. I only noticed this because I was such a clean freak myself, so I could see it in someone else, but the effect was one of total anonymity.

"I'm Eric," I extended my hand, but the red haired guy didn't respond. It was like making eye contact with a stuffed hunting trophy.

"You got a name?"

"You heard him," he said, "my name's Associate."

He held a cigarette to his mouth though I could have sworn his hand was empty and I didn't see him reach for his pocket.

"You can't smoke here," I said.

"It's not lit."

"Listen," I was doing my best to stay collected, "I've got a lot of combustible materials in there. I can't have anyone smoking within five hundred feet of the lab."

The Associate stooped to pick up a stone and said, "We're five hundred and twenty eight feet from your front door." He tossed the rock and said, "That's five hundred feet."

He had what I needed, though. My name was on nothing and any eyes tracing activity to and from the lab would die in the paperwork labyrinth White's Associate had created.

After Oz came Gotham. After Gotham came Valhalla. The network grew, as did the system for coding, concealing and signaling. Each crew knew their own set of codes, but I had to know them all. The bigger the network grew, the more we produced and the more I was left alone to work, but more room for error was introduced. If anyone in the network cut a corner or missed a step, the rogue molecules had a slim chance of either curing cancer or ending the world, but would most likely yield chemical waste that I'd end up paying for.

fifteen

THE TRUCK STOP COFFEE TASTED LIKE ACETONE BECAUSE THAT'S WHAT MY fingers smelled like when the lab work was finished. Two highway patrolmen took the opposite booth and I set my steaming cup down before my hands burst into quiet blue flame. I gave the waitress my order and went to scrub my hands again, then dialed my machine from the pay phone. The female android voice said, *You have. Twenty. Six. New messages.*

Twenty-six calls from a supplier who had my home number by mistake. Twenty-six calls from White. From Otto, the EPA or the DOJ. Twenty-six fires, subpoenas or arrest warrants. The solvents on my fingers mingled with the odor of cheap soap and the rotting sock stench of phosphorus.

You home yet? Okay, just seeing if you were. I'm working the promenade tonight, then I've got a street fair tomorrow. Call me as soon as you get back. Bye.

You scared me, Desiree.

Hey sweetie, you there? Hello? Pick up if you're there. Okay, I'm off to work. If you get this, just let yourself in and I'll be home by 11:00. I really want to see you.

Hey, where are you? Give me a call. Bye.

Eric. Call me. Just let me know when you're coming home.

Hey, I'm sorry I snapped. I know you're busy. I didn't mean to get so angry. I had a bad night, but I'm hoping the street fair will be better. I was hoping you'd be back so you could come with me. If you're not back now, then you probably won't be home until tonight. Late, right?

Hey you, I'm home. And you're not. Just call when you get this. No matter how late. Don't worry about waking me up, I just want to hear your voice.

I disconnected and dialed your number. Your machine picked up.

"Desiree, please stop calling. I'll be back tonight. I'm done working and I'm on the road. I stopped for lunch, but I'm heading out again and I'll be there as quickly as I can. Bye."

I asked the waitress to bag my order. The fear had blown through me like an electrical surge and shorted out my appetite. Maintaining composure while sipping coffee next to a pair of cops, with four ounces of refined red phosphorus inside my trunk, seemed like slow torture.

"Young man?"

My hand was on the diner door when the patrolman stopped me. "Officer?"

"That your car out there?"

My tags were good. The car was cherry, every light working and every window and mirror without a crack. I stank of the shitwater lab.

"The Ford." The cop dumped gravy onto a pile of potatoes.

"The '64, yeah, it's mine."

"You restore it yourself?"

Be cool. This guy might stop you, one day.

"Most of the engine work," I said.

"All original?"

"Salvage and stock." I glanced at my wrist, the one hint I knew to throw out before I said something stupid. I wasn't wearing a watch.

"The dashboard looked brand new."

"A guy in El Segundo did the work."

"I guess I don't need to say drive carefully. Have a good one."

"Thanks. Same to you."

The drive home could have been two hours or ten. It's a blur. The adrenaline rush faded somewhere around Twenty-Nine Palms as the stars were appearing overhead. I stopped for gas, changed my clothes in the restroom, ran a wet comb through my hair and washed my hands twice more.

You painted your bedroom purple, like the stained edges of morning glory petals, the darkest edge of the twilight sky, and I thought I was back outside with your window frame hanging midair.

"You're late. What do you think?"

The marks had been good to you. You'd painted the mirror's frame gold and covered an entire wall in velvet draperies. Your fortune-teller persona enveloped everything.

"I think it looks like a vampire whorehouse."

"I knew you'd like it. You'd better be hungry."

"I'm famished. I just don't feel like eating out."

"Good, because I'm cooking. Keep your coat on."

I'd been driving all day and had barely dropped my bag before we were out your door, again. You hadn't acknowledged your assault on my answering machine.

"What's that?"

"Guess." I tossed a frozen pizza into the grocery cart.

"I'm not buying frozen pizza."

"No, I am." The bright lights and piped-in music of the grocery store made my head hurt.

"Fine, but not for tonight. I told you I'm cooking. You like ahi, don't you?"

"Sure. I love ahi."

"Help me pick out some stuff for salad."

I picked a head of lettuce. You made a face, as though I'd fished it from a dumpster.

"You don't cook, do you?"

That depends on what you mean.

In an aisle below a COUGH & COLD REMEDIES sign, boxes upon bottles of pills and syrups promised new cures for old ailments. Marketing experts and focus groups point to colors—orange for pain, yellow for breathing, blue for sleep. PR firms run damage control when somebody spikes a random bottle. The warning labels grow longer, the print smaller. The laws change while the human body stays the same. Colds and headaches remain colds and headaches, and 95 percent of every pill on the market is inert binders and dyes.

The experts rig that 5 percent sweet spot with molecular detonator switches. Your solvent is off purity by 1 percent, your temperature wrong by a single degree, and you lose everything. They count on amateur cooks being discouraged, but they don't count on them being curious. For the curious, each failure shines another light onto the problem, which makes the slow diffusion of the chemical self-destruct mechanism so much sweeter when it's achieved, and there wasn't a pill on those shelves I couldn't pick apart, atom by atom, and pluck out precisely the atoms I needed.

The Buddha found enlightenment with Anaïs Nin, perched at the cracked spine of *Delta of Venus*. The jade deity belly laughed at the cosmic jokes the rest of us couldn't hear, turned luminous blue at the edges as I held my stare, unblinking, and the blue grew brighter, washing out your bookshelves, my bare feet propped on your couch, then the couch itself. The humming blue swallowed your curtains, your paintings and your twenty-six messages. It swallowed Pinstripe and his acid burns, the heated discussion with Manhattan White, my panic and the acetone stench wafting to the cops eight feet from me at the diner.

"Wash up," you said. "Dinner's ready." You dropped the plates with the same cold protest Mom made with Dad. The silence took me back home to my parents, to navigating the air of muted rage in our two-bedroom, evangelical pressure cooker.

Anyone knowing who I was could have sent me to prison for the combined contents of our shopping cart. You'd asked for distilled water. I picked up a bottle of mineral water. You put it back. Coffee filters, Epsom salts. For the split moment it takes for a fly's wings to beat, I thought you were on to me.

"Let's go. Now."

"I'm not finished. Just a minute." Your urgency for a romantic dinner was nowhere to be seen.

Iodine, bleach, rubbing alcohol, drain opener. Years of learning became discipline, discipline became habit. Habit became reflex and reflex became normal, not a reaction but my perpetual state of seeing. To convince me otherwise would be describing color to a blind man, water to a fish.

Who sent you?

"I am finished. And tired. I drove all day and would have been perfectly happy with a frozen pizza."

*

My hands smelled of sage and wildflowers from your soap. I dried them on a towel that smelled like your skin and hair, holding it to my face and breathing you in, amid the Mardi Gras beads, dried flowers, miniature framed photographs, eyebrow pencils and lipsticks in your bathroom. I folded the towel, felt the slightest feather touch against my eye and pulled one of your threads of fire from my face, a strand of sunlight.

You were washing the dishes.

"You need help with anything?"

You kept your back to me.

"Desiree?"

"Yes, Eric?"

"Do you need me to do anything?"

"No."

You curled onto your couch after dinner, your feet tucked beneath a blanket pulled tightly around you. The television's blue glow dulled your hair to a deep brown. I sat down beside you.

"Can I have some blanket, please?"

You relinquished a corner, without touching me. Your dog sat on a floor pillow, following our tense exchange and too timid to come too close to either of us.

You flipped channels, stopping on anything loud and full of laughter. You changed when feigning interest in a commercial exposed your cold shoulder for what it was. I knew this territory well. I could decorate cakes in a cancer ward if the circumstances warranted, but I didn't want to exhume my ghosts in your house.

We fought on the way home.

"What's wrong?"

"I just wanted to do something nice for you," you said. "I haven't seen you for days and you won't talk to me."

"I've been working, Dee. Nonstop. I don't want to talk about work."

"Then talk about something else."

"I don't have anything else."

"Ask me how I've been. Has that occurred to you? Or you could thank me for dinner."

"You haven't made dinner yet."

You pulled into a strip mall and parked next to a squad car.

"What are you doing?"

"I'm telling the cops about you," you said.

"Telling them what?" God help me, Desiree. I grabbed you. I held your wrist and your key ring scraped my arm.

"Let go of me."

"Telling them what?"

"Let go of me, you son of a bitch."

I let go.

"I'm telling them what a bastard you are," you said, and slammed the door.

The cop walked out of a liquor store, bench-press bulked and buzz cut. He set a deli sandwich onto his hood and popped open a bottle of orange juice. My first reaction was to reach for your keys but you'd taken them. You passed him without a word and entered an auto supply store. I stared at the floor of your car. You emerged three minutes later with two bottles of starter fluid.

"What's that?" I asked.

"Starter fluid, Mr. I Do My Own Engine Work."

"What for?"

Diethyl ether.

"My starter. What do you care?"

"You work on your own car?"

Coffee filters removed undissolved impurities. Epsom salts were for washing lab gear, their crystal structures trapped maverick water molecules, which could sabotage a controlled reaction.

"No, I don't," you said. "I can't do anything for myself. Except cook and clean. I need a big, strong man to take care of me. And I'm still looking for one."

You didn't protest when I turned off the television because you weren't watching it. You stared at the dead screen, out of ways to ignore me.

"Desiree, I didn't know you worked on your car." I reached for you, but you pulled away. "I didn't know because I didn't ask. I didn't ask how you've been and I didn't thank you for dinner. I'm sorry."

Choking back tears, your face twisted into a mangled mask. My forgotten phone calls and dodged questions added up to a signal I'd been oblivious to sending.

"You snapped at me in front of everyone at the grocery store. You yelled at me. You almost left a bruise."

"I didn't even realize I was doing it. I'm sorry. I really am."

"Why did you act that way?" Tears and snot.

"I don't have a reason. I was wrong. I was tired and didn't have any patience and I took it out on you."

"I just wanted to do something special for you. I just wanted you to call and talk to me. Just for a minute. That's all. I know you have work to do."

"Please stop it, Dee. You shouldn't have to explain yourself to me. Desiree, I'm sorry. I really am. I've been looking forward to seeing you since the minute I left. I haven't stopped thinking about you."

You opened your blanket to cover the two of us, your head resting in the crook of my neck so perfectly we could have been carved from the same block of marble. After a long silence, you asked for music and excused yourself. I put on Górecki's Third Symphony, one of your favorites, shut out the lights and lit a candle. You came back, wearing your underwear and one of my T-shirts. You blew the candle out.

"You don't like candles?"

"No."

"You're serious?"

"You can light it if you want. Just blow it out when we leave the room."

You wrapped around me, and we sat beneath the blanket listening to the sad symphony in the dark.

Somewhere, there's a part of me that knows right from wrong. That part of me, lying gagged and bound in my mental basement, still has enough breath to whisper through a spit-soaked gag that I should be protecting you, that if I fail every test of decency known to man, the fallout shouldn't come to you, that you had nothing to do with any of it. If I'm half a man, I should make certain you never know otherwise. I wanted to protect you, and if that made you angry with me, if it meant your never knowing why, then so be it.

All I need to do is patiently, one after the next, move one molecule from one place to another, one compound at a time, one failure after the next until something hits. It's a process of elimination. I used to work puzzles as a kid, and my mom taught me how to sort out the edge pieces first, assemble the frame, then apply that same process of elimination to all the remaining pieces. I could group them by color or pattern, whatever the picture was on the box. I learned to pick up each piece, one at a time, from my pile of potential matches and try to fit it from any angle into the socket, then discard it and move on. Each failure is meaningless. It's not me, it's the pieces, and I have to, absolutely must, try each and every piece every possible way until I find the one that fits. They aren't failures, they're steps, small bits of progress. I just needed to try moving one molecule at a time and I probably could have done it in your kitchen.

sixteen

I SLIP MY FINGERS BENEATH YOUR SHIRT TO THE SLICE OF FLESH ABOVE YOUR hips that feels so good in the dark but you hate so much. The places on you I love touching the most are the ones you like the least. Your touch fades. My dick feels like a prosthetic grafted onto me, devoid of sensation but heavy and rigid like a policeman's sap. I switch on the lamp and I'm miles above the earth, floating in the center of the galaxy with stars on all sides of me. How did I get here and where did you go? Ten slow breaths and the pale patches of wall come into focus, the square ghosts of the old pictures linger like the afterburn of sunlight when stepping into a dark room.

The bottle of nail polish is a knot of burning yellow from the heart of the sun. One of the stars moves and my brain regains footing. Legions of bugs cover the walls, ceiling and floor, each marked with yellow nail paint and glowing from the black light screwed into the lamp. They tagged me, so I tagged them back. There's nothing for them to report. I'm not doing anything but lying on my bed with my memories and my hard-on, but it looks like I'm floating in the middle of the universe. Shouting from the room next door, a crash against the wall startles the bugs and the constellations shift. Orion disbands, Scorpio dissolves, the galaxy crumbles.

I haven't slept in days, since I awoke to my empty brain and, in a blink, those days are gone. The time flies. The time flies feed on rotting clocks. The time flies are in collusion with the rest of the bugs. Each wave of fatigue brings a riptide of memory pulling me back. I kick against the current, gasping and choking for sleep, drowning in being awake, struggling to break the surface but the memory is too strong.

Hysteria comes in waves. Three-second surveillance loops of black gangbangers knocking over liquor stores boost the signals to earsplitting, tumor-inducing levels. Suburban teenagers cleaning out jewelry boxes and medicine cabinets do not. The transmissions are everywhere, ambient noise I cannot tune out, hard as I try. The frequency peaks and plummets with news of celebrity arrests, kidnapped white children and middle-class overdoses. Homeless addicts and crack-addled prostitutes drop dead daily by the score without a nod from the signals. A politician's son is arrested for possession and the signals go batshit. Everything on the street was birthed in the boardroom, patented and pumped into the public's bloodstream, one cure-all after the next. Then the snake oils went rogue, pitching housewives off ledges when their search for More hit a brick wall and they followed suit with the sidewalk. The saviors of spin rewrote history, and the epidemic of middle-class More became an epidemic of color and crime. The story repeated itself year after year, and I could set my watch to the pulsing of a fresh signal.

This one was different. One theory said it was an Alzheimer's treatment, another said it was for autism. They all said it was in the experimental stages and had somehow leaked to the streets and clubs. None of the reports could agree on what they didn't know.

One girl clamped herself into a fetal ball and screamed for hours before she opened her wrists in the bathtub. The paper said she'd suffered repeat violations from her stepbrothers as a child. They muffled her screams with a dishrag pushed into her mouth with a wooden spoon. Young women and men endured similar hallucinations, depending on their memories and experiences. Another boy shattered the bones in his fist, fighting off a string of imagined assailants and taking a swing at a fire door. Users described the sensation of fingers, hands, arms and lips. They felt the warm embrace of their mothers, the womb, an old lover, every stripper who dry humped their crotch, the first time they had sex, or the last. Sometimes the fingers were cold, like the unyielding grip of the dead, sometimes the caressing and stroking wouldn't stop.

They called it Skin, or Cradle. Derma was the fashionable variant, or "D." It went by different women's names in different circles, usually porn starlets. Some called it Pandora, some simply the Box. The slang hadn't settled. New street terms were sprouting more quickly than emergency room reports. The name depended on your experience, and some people never took it more than once.

The underground's new drug of choice gave concerned parents, waning politicians and preachers new fuel for their fury, opinion polls and collection baskets. The mob marching with their pitchforks and torches had no idea what they were marching against.

Hysteria drove demand and Hoyle would want a piece of it. If I knew what was good for me, I'd reverse engineer a sample before White came knocking. Staying out of a chicken wire blanket was good for me.

A kiss of sleep touches me on the eyes and my muscles go slack. Something bites me on the chest and I slap myself with the ferocity of a leather belt. Expecting to see a supernova splatter of bug entrails, smoking conductors and resistors in my palm, I only see dark. Even the constellations of starbugs and time flies are gone, the tickle of sleep frightened into a brain crevice like a feral cat. Another bite on the back of my neck. I stop midswing before I slap my bandages.

I climb from my bed and switch on the overhead light. My display of specimens grows, revealing everything and nothing, depending on how much nanowiring the bugs carry. Dark dots in the corners of my eyes bolt for the cracks and seams, but one freezes in place, trying to blend in, accustomed as he is to avoiding boot heels. I pick up the nail polish and move, keeping my vibrations to a minimum. It will dart for a crack once I'm too close, but I tag it with a quick brush to its back before it runs. I'm getting faster.

Red welts cover my chest, stomach and arms. I feel more on my back. God knows what bug spit is coagulating or eggs are incubating inside the bites, what kind of venom or infection is spreading or whether broken insect heads have lodged below the surface of my skin, feeding off me, growing new bodies, shitting into my bloodstream as they mature before taking flight out of an open sore. My skin burns. I need to shower and douse myself with vodka and boric acid and burn my sheets.

Someone is listening to me. The waking world floods at light speed through millions of neural checkpoints and one speck out of a billion screams doom. The cracking twig beneath the hunter's foot, the screaming child two floors below, the person outside my door.

My heart is like a small rabid rodent trying to claw through my lungs, an angry coke monkey locked in a cage, shrieking and climbing up and down my ribs because it keeps pressing the bell again and again and again but nothing's happening. I move, quiet as the gathering dust, through the labyrinth of creaking planks and press my ear to the door. I hear everything, like listening to the ebb and flow of millions of signals droning through the paper walls of a hornet's nest. The hissing of water pressure, the shuddering of faulty valves, footsteps above and below, the leaden clunk of soda cans falling from the vending machine, the coins tumbling through the slots, the twisting coils dropping peanuts or cigarettes. The television in the lobby and a hundred others throughout the Firebird, sitcom laugh tracks, car chase tire squeals, crowds going wild, which sound like big bang static from the dead screens the junkies left on before they passed out. I hear the fights, the phone calls, the electricity humming and shorting, voices and bugs clinging to the two-by-four studs, others chewing their way through and the rats shaving away at the foundation of the hotel, battling the ants for real estate. This is how the Firebird sounds to God.

A sting shoots up the nerves in my leg. I scratch through my pants, hoping to crush the bastard crawling up to my crotch. The dead leather rope tail of a rat slaps my bare foot, the little monster claws gripping my outer arch before it scurries away. I brush my foot against the calf of my jeans, wiping away the tingle from the rat's tail, and look for the hole where that little bastard rodent comes and goes like it owns the place, when my doorknob moves. Hold very still. Pressing my ear to the door again and the noises come flooding back. This time, my whispered name brushes my ear like a feather. The voice smells me listening, I know it. The doorknob moves when I look away, then stops when I look back. He's good, quiet as my own shadow. The cops would kick my door off the hinges, God style. The Firebird junkies would wait until I'd left to rip me off. Somebody planted the bugs in here and knows my every move. Somebody out there wants me when I'm in here.

Toe Tag.

Shit.

Goddamned Boo Radley with a chloroform rag and a bone saw.

The knob moves again, the faintest tick like a spider trapped inside the tumbler. The rabid lab weasel locked in my chest fights with the coked-up monkey, both tearing at my insides and shrieking in my ears.

The television will go through the door if I have a running start. Those three or four or five steps might give me away, but Toe Tag won't expect me to get the drop on him. All I need is an unconscious Toe Tag on the hallway floor, lock pick in one hand and piano wire in the other, to clear things with Anslinger.

I sprint, screaming Fuck you, Boo Radley, and the airborne television's cord catches my wrist, nearly ripping my arm from the socket. I'm waving through the splintered hole in my door, my hand turning purple from the power cord cinched around the wrist but the hallway is empty. Goddamn, he's fast.

seventeen

I'm having a tough time explaining this to Anslinger. As well as being on the Warden's shit list, I'm in deep with the Firebird residents. A crashing door sounds like the apocalypse to them, and a visit from the law suspends all activity, the buying, selling, shooting and bartering. The Firebird's lifeblood freezes for a window as crippling as it is brief.

"I do a birth record search on 'Toe Tag,' what am I going to find?"

Anslinger wears black today. The kerchief tucked into his front pocket shifts between blue and green when he moves beneath the light. He scans my brain tissue while a pair of plainclothes cops wearing rubber gloves toss my room. They pile their plunder atop my mattress—my clothes, bug spray, yellow marking paint, boric acid, steel wool. They tag my notebook, drop it into a property envelope. A uniform takes notes while we speak. Another snaps pictures of my dissections and diagrams. They're new to the force, straight from the assembly line. Their fresh static burns my nose and makes my eyes water but my hands are cuffed.

"I'm sure it's a nickname," I say. "That name can't be real."

"You've got great instincts, my man. This retarded savant killer couldn't possibly have a name like that."

"I've seen him."

"You mean you think you remember meeting him."

"No, I've seen him," I insist. "Some details are crystal clear. Others are sketchy. Things are coming to me but it's hard. Does this make me cooperative or not?"

"If I come to you, that makes you uncooperative, but my disposition can change depending on what I learn from you. I'm in a good mood today," he says, "so I'll cut you some slack in this particular instance. Tell me more. Who looks after this short bus assassin?"

Toe Tag works the muscle for the chain with his stun gun, syringes, plastic bags, draining shunts, bolt cutters and bone saws. He answers to his father, Manhattan White, a ranking executive in the chain that funded the lab. White runs things according to Hoyle's instructions, who controls the chain and its assets. I started out experimenting and they pulled me in. The money was good and it was supposed to be short-term.

Anslinger leans against the wall, wetting the filter of a fresh cigarette between his lips, James Dean cool. His lighter chimes like a round snapping into a chamber. His tape recorder stares at me with its glowing red eye, a lump of primitive mechanics and magnetic tape. He must think I'm insane to fall for such a cheap decoy.

A field medic examines my bandages, runs a gloved fingertip over the bites on my arms, then swabs one in the crook of my elbow with alcohol.

"Are they infected? Maybe I'm having an allergic reaction."

"These aren't insect bites." He addresses Anslinger instead of me.

The uniform reads my statement, unable to keep a straight face. A bug clamps onto my arm, I think, but it's the medic shooting something into my vein.

"Easy," he says.

"What's that?" I ask.

"Thank you, doctor," says Anslinger, but the man's not a doctor and Anslinger isn't paying idle courtesy. He's sending a high-frequency signal that everyone catches at once, everyone but the rookies. The rubber glove cops drop everything and exit without a word. The field medic slaps his kit shut and leaves without bandaging my leaking injection point. The rookies stand bewildered, not tuned to Anslinger's wavelength of command. In two swipes, Anslinger rips the notebook and camera from their hands, like pulling the cloth from beneath a banquet setting. He dismisses them both.

The room is empty but for Anslinger and me. The warden's handyman removed the television and the remains of my door. I hear murmuring from the hallway.

Anslinger crouches to my level. He locks his brown eyes onto mine and stares through to the inside of my head. Blood moves to my brain, fueling my thoughts. Anslinger can read the heat patterns with those eyes. He needs neither a tape recorder nor some rookie's notes or pictures. Here comes his Big Speech, I think, but he smiles, stands and leaves.

Something bites my chest. I hunch my shoulders to scrape it with my chin but it's too low. It severs its tracking chip head into my bloodstream then crawls deaf, blind and leaking around my belly, down my back and drops out my shirttail. It sounds like a bottle cap hitting the floor.

My notebook slaps the desk, freed from its brown envelope and one-way ticket to the evidence locker.

"If it were up to me, I'd beat your ass into the dirt," the uniform says. The name below his badge reads "Officer Lloyd Delgado." The note taker.

It's not up to you, I think, though I have the sense not to say it out loud.

"It's your lucky day." He hisses into my ear with a voice like a blown speaker. "He must really like you." As he unlocks my cuffs, he torques my wrist until pain shoots up my arm.

"How do you know?"

"Because I know when he doesn't."

I massage the feeling back into my arm. Officer Delgado, Anslinger and everyone else are gone, as though they silently faded into nothing.

The warden steps into my doorway, his jaw set. If he doesn't kick me out, it means Anslinger had a talk with him.

"You need anything?" he asks.

"A door."

"I know you need a door." He looks to his left and right, then speaks in a low voice. "You bring that kind of heat here again, they'll be carrying you out." He leaves.

The warden's handyman, wearing work gloves and a canvas tool belt, props a door in the hallway outside, a spare that's been collecting dust and mildew in the basement.

"I hear you've got a bug problem," he says.

eighteen

ONE OF WHITE'S STUTTERING LAB GEEKS GAVE WORD THAT A COYOTE BY THE handle of High Tail had gone supernova between drops, scorching his ghost onto a patch of Route 127 like a Nagasaki flash shadow. I was carrying four pounds of lysergic acid amides in my trunk when I stopped to check my messages from a gas station pay phone. Otto was wiping dragonfly guts from my windshield when I heard the black magic word assigned to the signal man working Gotham.

"Hindenburg." Dial tone.

A Wicker Man could be contained. A Hindenburg meant an accident en route, so the highway patrol knew about it first. My Gotham man had been on point, ears glued to the scanner, but he'd been taking payment in product to stay awake. His panic was contagious.

The signal man picked up on the first ring.

"Go," he said. Emergency phone protocol. Say nothing explicit and keep it short.

"Yes or no," I said. "Nothing else. Is Angela there?"

"Yes."

If a tapeworm in the phone picked up the name, it wouldn't matter. Angela was code—wipe everything down.

"Cargo."

"I didn't—"

"Cargo."

"No."

They should have packed while waiting for me to phone. The drill called for the crew to load their belongings—nobody brought more than a single bag—wipe everything down, salvage the product, abandon the glass and cut our losses.

"Then everyone pack up and walk," I said. "And I mean walk. Do you understand?"

"There's—"

"Do you understand?"

"Yes."

"Product?"

"No."

"You know where to whisper?"

"Tell me," he said.

"I'll tell you when you get there."

"In thirty."

"Twenty." I hung up.

Once the authorities ID'd our dead man, they'd run his arrest sheet, bank and credit card action, phone records and every pay phone within a mile of his residence, and repeat the same for his known associates and lean on every one of them with both barrels. Delinquent parking fines, outstanding warrants, parole violations, child protective services, property search and seizure, rat jackets.

Somebody always talks. Always. The cops dangle immunity deals and cash payouts from seized trafficking assets. Nobody gets cuffed and stuffed solo, and every one of them knows someone else, their best friend, wife or children, who will break in exchange for the free ticket out and a marked bankroll. They had to be faster than the next guy, so our crews had to be faster than the DMV and dental records.

*

We were en route from Texas. I'd grown a culture of claviceps fungus at Gotham, then moved it via coyote to a location code-named Sleepy Hollow, where the crew used it to infect a rye crop. Otto and I arrived just after their midnight harvest. I worked with them until sunrise pulverizing the seeds and showing them how to leech out the fats with toluene. The resulting black mash was sensitive to light, air and temperature change, so I triple sealed it on dry ice before I hit the road. On certain runs, I prefer my own wheels. I didn't want one of White's idiots veering into a reservoir or river. The call from Gotham confirmed my caution.

One cook was legend. His blotter sheets were ready for infusion when he did a face-plant in his own lab. A puddle, a stray cord or a six pack, no one will ever know. He splashed a quart of pure, liquid LSD all over himself as his head hit the concrete. He went black for a week. To this day, he swears he reinvented acid, but his girlfriend's dog was a spy for the government who stole the recipe and engineered his accident.

I left the crew their cash and instructions to dismantle the lab and abandon Sleepy Hollow. I'd been driving ever since. We had to store the ice chest at Gotham until runners arrived with the other materials. I was anxious to get home, Otto was anxious to hit the Vegas tables for an afternoon.

Otto reached into the car and flashed the headlights. I waved him off. He resumed cleaning the windows. Wasps, crickets, moths, locusts and horseflies grew bigger the deeper into Texas we drove. Where men are men and so are the insects, he'd said. They hit my windshield at 70 mph like small rocks, held on long enough to crack out the whiplash then flew away. Others exploded on impact, their guts blotting out an entire headlight.

After eighteen minutes, I dialed the second pay phone. The signal man answered, sucking wind.

"Go."

"Your turn," I said. I needed details.

"Who is this?"

"You said, 'Hindenburg,' that's who. Tell me everything is sprayed and the glass broken."

"It's done. But they wanna get paid and they're scared. And pissed."

"If you shut down and dispersed according to procedure, you having nothing to worry about. Everyone will get paid, but they'll have to wait."

"I heard about the last one."

"You heard what?"

"Pinstripe."

"Shut up." I listened to the wire hum. Tapeworms don't click, like the old days. They're quieter. Alias or not, he said Pinstripe's name. His crew wasn't connected with Pinstripe's crew. The coyotes didn't know each other or the cargo they carried.

"The guy," the signal man was stuttering, "he was getting help and nobody's seen him."

"Who told you that?"

"I heard."

From a rogue link in the chain.

"Listen, he screwed up," I said. "He didn't follow instructions and had to get help. He's fine, but he's out of the crew. That's why nobody's heard from him."

I'd forgotten about Pinstripe as soon as I passed him off to White.

"Now, pull it together and tell me what happened."

The coyote was carrying phosphorus. Someone overpacked. Someone left impurities in the product. The agitation on the drive created a spark. The CHP found the smoking husk of the VW, the paint blistered from the heat, in the middle of the road, overturned from the driver's attempt to regain control after the spontaneous combustion of the cargo. He drove the flaming ball for a quarter mile of absolute panic before rolling it, setting off the gas tank and the rest of the cargo.

God, how I missed you then.

A week ago, you blocked my way into your front door after I'd just returned from another road trip.

"Tell me you missed me," you said.

"I missed you."

Maybe I didn't look you in the eye long enough. Maybe my tone was off, ever so slightly.

"Try again," you said. "And mean it."

"I missed you," I said again. "I came straight here. I haven't been home because I wanted to see you first."

You smiled, weighing my sincerity against its expression. You stepped aside to let me through. I dropped my bag and pulled you to me, burying my face in your flaming hair.

"I did miss you, Firefly."

"Don't call me that." You took my wrist and pulled me inside.

"I could do this forever," I said. You squeezed me, lightly. "Just lie here beside you. Watch the sun go down."

"How can the sun go down forever?" Your voice sleepy.

"Sorry?"

"You said you could do this forever." You rested your chin on me. Your eyes were brighter.

"And then you said you could watch the sun go down. How can you do both?"

"I try to be romantic and you mince words."

"Giving you a hard time," you said, then kissed my chest.

"Maybe the sun could set really slowly. I mean really take its time."

"Sshhhh."

Darkness settled. Your curtains open, no moon in the sky. We'd kicked the covers away in the heat, and I wanted to look at you.

"Where are you going?" you asked.

"Bathroom. I'll light a candle when I get back."

"Hurry back. No candles," you said into your pillow.

I thought you were joking until I struck a match.

"Eric, I'm serious. Don't."

"Once again, I'm the romantic one."

You said nothing, your face away from me.

"Hey. Your house burn down or something?" Your room grew darker in the silence. "I'm sorry."

"It's okay."

"No, it's not."

"You didn't know. It's just my stupid hang-up."

"It's not stupid."

"It's stupid. I'm paranoid, and that's stupid."

"You're paranoid about fire in general or just candles? Is that how your house burned down?"

"No, that's the stupid part. It was a fire in our kitchen when I was four years old. My mom was cooking. But I've been really sketchy about some things ever since. I hate gas stoves. Candles didn't always bother me, really, until an old roommate of mine started a fire in our apartment. She was stoned."

"You've had two homes burn down."

"No, the second time wasn't serious. She lost a bunch of her stuff to smoke and water damage. But when I was little, our family lost everything. Nobody got hurt, but everything was gone."

"Where were you?"

"I was watching the parade."

"What parade?"

"We lived near a middle school and their marching band would practice around our neighborhood. I used to run outside because I thought it was a parade. My own parade, every day."

"You were saved by a marching band."

"After my roommate started the fire in our apartment, I think I freaked. I don't remember, but I definitely overreacted. Then she told them about me, so this asshole fireman thought he could get into my pants. He got our number and kept asking me out. I said no for three weeks before he gave up. Guys were always saying they had gone through the training or were thinking about becoming firemen. Like I was some damsel in distress who's going to get wet over firemen."

"When it's really marching bands that get you hot."

"Go home." You hit me with a pillow.

"I'm going to learn the trombone."

"You're a jerk."

"And wear one of those shiny hats."

"They're called shakos."

"Busted."

You hit me again.

"Forget it," I said. "I'm going whole hog and learning the tuba."

"Good. The standup lessons aren't paying off." You left for the bathroom. I loved watching you in the dark.

Your body jigsaw wedged against mine when I woke, your face against my neck and our ankles interlocked, the morning glow of your room turning into the garish sunlight I'd be driving through, to Texas and back. You were asleep, but still clung fast when I tried to get out of bed. The hot shower pounded me awake and I ran through my departure checklist. I gave myself five days for the round trip.

I leaned over to kiss you before I left, and you pulled away.

"Do you have to leave again?"

"Yes."

"Can't you wait for a day?"

"No. Please, let's not get into that."

"One day."

"Please," I said. "It's my turn to be serious. Please don't harass me about work. I'll call you, every day. At least once, I promise."

"Promise me."

"I just did."

"Say it again."

"I promise. I'll call you every day."

"Thank you."

"Can I still call you Firefly?"

You nodded.

"Then go to sleep, Firefly." I kissed you and left.

Otto honked the horn, impatient, though still cleaning the windows.

"You're taking up too much space on my machine," I said. "I promised I would call."

"You didn't call all day."

"I promised I would call," I said once more. "And I did. I haven't had time today, so I'm doing it now."

"You were too busy to make a single phone call?"

I was too busy to make a single phone call that would log your number into a pay phone that could, at some point, be audited.

"Yes, I was. And I have to go now."

"Okay." Your cold pout came all the way through the lines.

"Dee, I miss you. I want to see you and I'd much rather be there than here. Please. I'll be back as soon as I can."

"Just come straight over."

"I'll stop at home, shower and then be straight over."

"You can shower here. I washed the clothes you left."

"Okay." Anything to end this conversation. "I'll go straight to your place. But please, no more messages while I'm out of town."

The horn honked, the headlights flashed. We said our good-byes.

The electric red-eye blink on my machine flashed fourteen times in the dark, paused, then cycled through again. I was too jaded to panic. I dialed the relay number for White, hung up, then heard the footsteps outside. Someone knocked, or I heard the tapping and creaking of my settling house. Someone whispered my name, or I heard the breeze brushing leaves against the windows. I sat in the dark, waiting for my windows to explode and the dark soldiers to fly through the glass, their lights in my eyes and gun barrels to my head.

I'm a boy again, hiding beneath my covers from the monsters in my room, the deformed and disfigured faces I see in the tree bark at night are leaning over me, waiting for me to breathe.

*

I'm on my bed at the Firebird. So are you. I'm safe.

Another knock.

"Eric?"

No mistaking my name, this time.

The peephole distorted your face. I unlocked the three deadbolts and flung the door open. You stepped back, startled.

"What are you doing here?"

"You said you'd come to my house first."

"Keep your voice down. I wanted to, but I had to stop."

"For what?"

"I said keep your voice down."

"Why won't you let me in?"

"Desiree, please be quiet."

"I'll talk as loud as I want if you're going to make me stand on the goddamned porch."

I grabbed your wrist and pulled you inside. You started to shout and I clamped my hand over your mouth.

"Okay, you're inside. Now keep your voice down."

"Why did you do that?" You were rubbing your wrist. The fear and sadness twisted your face until you looked twenty years older in the faint light. "You don't have to be so mean." The words squeezed from your throat, wrapped around a sob.

"Why can't you give me some breathing room? What the Christ gives you the right to stampede through my life like this? Who do you think you are?"

It broke my heart to break yours. The bulldog facade that served in my dealings with White served only to hurt you, and I lost sight of that between my road fatigue and rabbit hole focus.

"I want to be special." You were crying. "You're always gone and I know you drive for your job and I worry about you."

"Don't."

"I want to. I thought maybe you would worry about me if I were going somewhere like you do. But you don't call. I've never even been here before. You've never asked me to your house and you act like you don't even live here. There's nothing here and I don't know if you're telling me the truth. I just wanted to be special. I thought you liked me."

"Dee, you're special, please."

"Fuck you. If I'm so special then tell me where you go for your job. Why does it look like you haven't even moved in? What are you doing that's so secret?"

"Nothing. Desiree, please stop shouting."

"Quit saying that and tell me what you're doing." Your face was slick from crying. You wiped your nose with your fingers.

"I'll get you a tissue."

"I want to know."

"You don't lower your voice and I'm going to tape your god-damned mouth shut."

"You touch me again and I'm calling the police."

I owe you what happiness I had, in what little of my life I can recall. It stands to reason that I owe you my life but, at the very least, I owe you an explanation.

You would settle for nothing less than being completely woven into my life, which meant crossing threads with Hoyle. Segmenting you from my life with the chain was pursuing a mirage, perpetually within sight while perpetually out of reach. Hoyle would find you. You weren't safe if you didn't stay away from me, and you wouldn't stay away from me if you didn't hate me. You couldn't hate me if you weren't afraid of me. I backed down once in the face of your anger, I couldn't back down again.

Your eyes were wide and unblinking when I slapped my hand over your mouth, a strip of duct tape in my palm.

Your skin fades from mine like a dimming shadow. You're gone. I open my eyes and the leaden, gray forever returns, crushing my room. I'm drying up, coming down. Ride it out. Reload. I know my rhythm.

My pants unbuttoned, my shirt folded, one shoe on but the other dangles from my fingers. A minute passes, a day. Was I taking my shoes off or putting them on? Look at my hand, remember looking at my hand, remember remembering looking at my hand. Follow the seconds backward. Another minute passes, another day. Was I taking my shoes off or putting them on?

I'm at the Firebird.

Your name is Desiree.

The last thing I remember, I'd covered your mouth and lashed your wrists with silver tape. I sat on your knees until you quit fighting me.

I was putting my shoes on, leaving to reload.

The Glass Stripper isn't dancing. Come back later, says the Token Man. Every clock in the world is frozen. The tentative light of either sunrise or sunset mutes the glow and the shadows from the street-lamps.

*

Three jack and Cokes from Lou.

I shove a wad of bills to the Glass Stripper and ask for it all.

My memory was wrong. It was a game. Your pale, naked body slashed the dark, lashed to the legs of my furniture and tensed tight as a coiled snake but too frightened to move, a strip of gray across your eyes, your frozen inferno of copper-colored hair splayed across my wood floor.

The last thing you said was "How do I know I can trust you?"

"You don't. That's why it's called trust." I covered your mouth with tape after that, after I'd tied you down, not before.

I wrapped an insulator blanket around a drip flask, which I connected with glass pipe to an Erlenmeyer flask over a heating coil. With a liter of water between them, and the temperature kept at a constant, the pressure forced out a single, warm drop three feet above your bare crotch, one drop every five seconds, tap, tap, tap.

I sat on my floor in the dark and watched.

When the first drop hit, your legs stayed taut, a strip of sweat shining the length of both thighs, and you shook your head as though trying to look around you, trying to see something through your blindness. The second and third drops hit and you stopped moving, and the sweat shine circled your heaving belly and your legs tensed with each fresh smack from the flask. The liter could last five hours.

The sweat highlighting your body looked like firefly trails on your skin. After an hour, you were swollen pink and arching your hips in the dark, willing the tap to come faster. I walked barefoot, holding my breath, and caught one of the drops in my palm. You squirmed, hungry for the liquid tickle and the anticipation made you swell even more and you moaned.

I caught nine drops in my palm and let the tenth one fall, then eight and let the last two fall, then seven. When I returned to a full ten drops in a row, your skin had flushed pink from head to toe, feverish and hot, and I began the cycle again. I widened the choke on the flask so the drops were fatter, came slower and hit harder. I caught a few more warm, falling drops and distorted your rhythm, left you thrashing above the growing wet circle below your ass.

The phone rang, the electronic chirp killing the mood and distracting you. I was expecting White.

"Go."

I whispered while White spoke.

"I heard," he said. "Tell me it's under control."

"It is. Do likewise."

"About what?"

There were days, most of them, when I wanted to kill Manhattan White.

"About our Wicker Man."

"I'm not following you." He spoke with his mouth full. I heard a television in the background.

"Either follow me, or talk to me at work."

"You mean you can't talk."

No, I can't. My girlfriend's naked, blindfolded, gagged and tied with duct tape on my living room floor.

"Exactly. Now, what's his story? The rest of the employees are worried and it's a distraction."

"You setting me up to say something?" He was laughing.

"We had a problem," I said, "and I called you for help. I need to know what shape our problem is in."

"There is no problem. You called us in to take care of the problem and we did."

"Christ." My mouth went dry. I'd held Pinstripe's arm and helped him into the van. "Not like that. You can't be serious."

"Check your spine, boy." The chewing stopped. I heard a door close, shutting out the television sound. "Stop deluding yourself. What did you think we were going to do? What do you think happens when you call us in an emergency? Problems sing, and they sing loud. You there?"

I'm here.

"Say you're there."

"Here."

"Our recent episode. I don't need to worry, do I?"

"It's been wished into the cornfield," I said. "Everything's gone. I'm just keeping you up to speed."

"And I appreciate that," he said. "You're doing a tremendous job. I should tell you that more often."

"Right. Thanks."

"And stop worrying. You did the right thing. And I know you always will."

"Time," I said. White hung up first.

I slid the phone away as your body seized up, the veins on your face and neck standing out until I thought they would burst. You were breathing so heavily through your nose I felt my own heart, like it was beating for the first time in hours. I stripped the tape from your lips and kissed you and you started sobbing out loud.

"I love you, Firefly. You are the center of the universe, to me. I won't let anything happen to you."

nineteen

HOYLE WANTED SKIN AND HOYLE'S WORD WAS FINAL. WHITE WANTED AN explanation because White wanted to cover his ass. What was it made from, how and by whom, he wanted to know. You're experimenting, White said, how did somebody beat us to it? Hoyle had made his directive. Otto and I were fish food if we didn't deliver, our remains digested and served up on roadside diner specials, our skeletons in a chicken wire coffin.

More news reports were hitting the air and rebounding off middle-class fears and I knew, as did White, as did Hoyle, that for every account of somebody dropping dead or having convulsions in an emergency room, there were five hundred people who hadn't, and every one of those people who didn't had paid anywhere from five to twenty bucks for a hit.

"So you're on top of this, right?" White kept putting me on hold, picking up, asking me questions and then cutting me off.

"You mean, did I see this coming? Or do you mean can I stop everything I'm doing now to chase this stuff down and save your ass with Hoyle?"

"I mean you need to call me in five days and tell me you know what it is and how to make it."

"I'm not going to tell you that. I'm going to need a sample in order to isolate the active ingredient or ingredients, and see if I can identify them. And if I can, that's *if*, there's the questions of synthesizing it."

"Shouldn't you be out tracking down this sample?"

"You're joking, right? You don't even have that?"

"Why would I?"

"I had this silly notion that maybe, just maybe, you had your hands on an actual dose or doses of the stuff that's making headlines and that you want to start manufacturing. That's just me."

"Call me when you accomplish something." White hung up.

The fruits of my labors surrounded me but I wanted nothing to do with them and they wanted nothing to do with me. The club was in a converted warehouse, and the linebacker-sized doormen sporting earpieces and clipboards were giving me the cold shoulder.

"Guest list on the right, everybody else on the left."

Bribing them was a waste of time. I was older than most of the clubgoers and didn't have safety pins, nail heads and stereo nobs hanging off my face. My utilitarian civilian wear tagged me as a cop and the irony wasn't lost on me but I wasn't feeling the humor, either. I'd be waiting in the non-guest-list line all night as they bumped gaggles of girls and teenage actors ahead of me.

I paid some girl in pigtails and glowing armbands sucking on a lollipop to hang with me in line.

"What's your name?" I asked. She told me and I immediately forgot.

"You're a cop, aren't you?"

Neither my yes or no would change her mind. I was tempted to say yes, just to mess with her but I didn't want that rumor started.

"No, I'm just not as fashionable as everybody else."

She still thought I was a cop but, in the spirit of global unity and fighting the establishment, she accepted three hundred bucks to hang on my arm when we reached the front of the line, flap her eyelashes at the doorman and make certain I got in with her.

I was going deaf from the music and the subwoofers were making me nauseous. The sound system half-ass jury-rigged through the warehouse, lights over the bar and strobes and fog machines—all the electricity made my brain tingle and I could hear the static, smell it and taste it on my tongue like licking a nine-volt battery, and I was parched.

I spent an hour lurking at the bar, looking more suspicious with each passing minute, wondering how to approach someone. I'd pressed thousands of pounds in tablets at Oz, but didn't have the faintest clue how they were scattered at street level. For all I knew, I'd end up buying from some low-level ant who shared the same chain I did. Some kid approached me with no finesse whatsoever, and asked me for ecstacy.

"Sorry," I said. "I'm looking myself."

I asked him if he knew anyone holding Cradle and he laughed. The answer was either no, or I was using the wrong name, or both. Things came too easily or not at all. Everyone who thought I wasn't a cop thought I was some civilian they could dupe. As it turned out, I was wrong about witnessing the fruits of my labor. Most everything I managed to score was a crumbling, poorly pressed tablet with cheap dye that stained my palms. One after the next, I cracked tablets with my thumbnail and I smelled safron or lactose or too much of one thing or another. Everybody said, yeah, I know what you're looking for, but they didn't. They thought I was a mark. Back at the bar, some girl with a chrome pin through her tongue and eyes with pupils swollen wide from a battery of drugs leaned into me and said, "You want some Touch?"

I was barely keeping up with the name. I nodded, my instincts telling me I wouldn't have to come back the next night. I wanted to get out of there. All that electricity was making me thirsty.

*

Otto hadn't picked up the phone at Oz since I'd returned. I almost caved and abandoned callback protocol, just to get through and quit worrying. This is how people ended up in jail or dead. No, I had to call the main line at the lab, let it ring once, call back and let it ring twice. After ten minutes, I'd call the pay phone down the road, the one in the pristine glass booth at the phantom gas station where he'd be waiting. He wasn't, and this was the beginning of my worry. People had to be on time, they had to be where and when they were assigned.

I'd left him behind because he wanted to hit Vegas, while I still needed to get back home. I pointed out he had no car and he said not to worry, so I didn't, but I wish I had. I needed him now. Because of my impulsive attempt to douse your fury, I found myself with no way back to Oz since I'd left you the Galaxie to drive to your parents' for the weekend.

"How you doin'?" he asked. He was a kid, a little younger than me, dressed more subdued than the other kids at the club, but still looking like an idiot with the fishing hat and wraparound glasses. The girl I'd met at the bar introduced us.

"Spectacular," I said.

"You a cop?"

"No."

"You affiliated with the law or law enforcement in any way?"

I could have broken his heart and told him that the question didn't matter. I figured somebody else would, and that somebody would be carrying a set of cuffs and a microphone wired to a battery below his nutsack.

"No I'm not affiliated with the law or law enforcement in any way."

"Aren't you kind of old to be hanging out in a place like this?"

"I've got money," I said, wanting to get this over with. "I'm looking for as many hits of Touch as you can get me, without getting yourself in trouble. Right now, cash. If you've got it, then talk to me, otherwise don't waste my time. I'm buying. Just in case your microphone didn't pick that up."

"Easy," he said, "I ain't no cop. How much you looking for?"

"I'm looking for as much as I can get." He lit up when he saw my load of bills. My last stop at Oz, I'd made another deposit to the bank, neatly stacking and ordering the bills sequentially, but I took out my salary before heading back home.

In a men's room stall, he handed me a piece of intricately folded Christmas wrapping and said, "This is all I've got with me, but there's more. You ever tried it?"

I shook my head and opened the makeshift envelope.

"There's nothing like it," he said.

I let one of the tablets drop into my palm. It was expertly pressed with no markings and buffered to a glossy blue, the color of your eyes.

"Blue Fireflies," he said, "or just 'Fireflies.'"

Indeed, they were fireflies. I know, because I made them.

twenty

I CALLED WHITE TO TAKE ME BACK TO OZ. WE HARDLY SPOKE FOR THE ENTIRE drive. I couldn't shake the feeling that he'd love to see me fail and have his son feed me to the fish.

"Where's your boy?" I asked, but he said nothing. Idiotic small talk and he knew it. He knew I didn't care, that I didn't like his son and that the sight of him sickened me. I said "your boy" instead of "Toe Tag." As well as the name fit, I couldn't bring myself to use it.

I leaned against the window and closed my eyes, not to sleep, but to avoid the silence and stilted conversation. When I'd open my eyes, I'd find White staring at me in the dark, oblivious to the road, with the oncoming headlights bouncing off his eyes.

Three silent hours later, we pulled up to the gate at Oz. I'd installed a transmitter in the hinge that set off a signal when it opened, so I knew from inside, with a three-hundred-yard warning, that somebody was coming through.

"I'll see you in a few days," I said.

White sped off and left me standing in a wake of airborne dirt, my overnight bag in one hand and my free hand clutching at my collar to ward off the cold.

I sat on Oz's porch and thought about how much of my life happened on porches and thresholds: me and Dad taking pictures of fireflies and the stars, you and I drinking wine and watching the sun go down, my first experiments. I was always in front of a house or below it, but never in one, except yours. Never anywhere. Ask me to describe where I live to you and I couldn't.

My reverie was interrupted by a barking dog, one that sounded remarkably like your yipping, high-maintenance monster, coming from inside the house.

I opened up and there it was, jumping up and down in the dark and excited as all hell to see me and I couldn't figure out why. Regardless, I was pissed to see it and as loathe as I am to use lights in the main house at night, I did because I was even more loath to step into a pile of neglected canine shit.

I couldn't smell anything and I scanned the bright, empty room for telltale piles but saw nothing while the creature yapped and yapped at my ankles. In the kitchen, a layer of the *Los Angeles Times* was spread out, the sports section, with a shiny coil covering some NFL player's head. An empty bowl that smelled vaguely of beef residue sat in the corner beside another bowl of water.

The note from Otto said, "We've got our guard dog until she wants him back. See you in a couple of days." I wanted to kill them both. I had work to do and the beast was going to make noise, want to play, spill shit and draw attention and I couldn't let him outside otherwise he'd be coyote meat.

I found a bag of dog food in the cupboard and refilled his bowl, rolled up the newspaper, threw it in the outside trash, and put a fresh sports page down. Tomorrow, he'd be tethered outside with whatever I could find. For now, I opened a can of soup from the pantry, ate, showered and went to the basement lab to salvage what I could from my notes.

The entrance to the basement from the outside was via a storm cellar door, but it was bolted from the inside. Within the house, a door in the kitchen led down a set of concrete stairs into the lab that was still my favorite work space.

I needed time. I was fried from the drive with White and I had to sleep, just a little. Otto was gone and I was on my own. I could sew it up, reverse-engineer the compounds after I'd isolated their active alkaloids. I didn't have to produce the drug, I just had to be able to tell White and Hoyle that I knew how, and without them knowing the stuff was mine to begin with. They weren't stupid, they'd figure it out on their own, regardless, but I've found the best way to play politics is to not play them at all, that the truth would be the shortest route to my safety. Yes, I'd been experimenting and they knew that, but the notes were destroyed in the fire caused by the crew I hadn't wanted to hire in the first place.

Oz was a cubicle, now, a small, gray square of partitions with my calendar and company coffee mug, pertinent memos tacked beside my computer. I was pacing, tapping my fist against my palm and mumbling out loud while the stupid dog stared at me for some attention, flapping its tail. Eat, sleep, run, bark, shit, eat and sleep. A walking ball of appetites indulged, an existence that most of us will never know because in the case of this little monster, someone was there to take care of it. I checked the locks on the doors, then went over my notes as I lay on the couch, hoping to sleep a while.

A line of white dust was the embodiment of More and the first wave hit me in seconds, my whole body and not my brain, more of everything. More energy, more awake, more ideas, more brainstorms and more happiness. The obstacles hadn't changed, I still had days ahead of me in the desert Oz, but I could do it. More of you, Desiree. I was filled with a bottomless love for you that I always knew was there but had never tapped into and it was leaking out of every pore and I wanted to laugh at the sun and the sky and every bug crawling along the Mojave dirt because it was all so much and so little at the same time.

Everything was going to be okay. I would figure things out, bail myself out of trouble and practically print money for Hoyle and then, Dee, you and I would vanish, go wherever we wanted. Get that red-haired Associate guy to set us up and never see the inside of the lab again unless I wanted to, when I wanted to. I promised, I could make everything better because I knew I could, because I was feeling it right then and mother of God, it was good. I wouldn't make it a habit, and I knew those were famous last words but as good as it felt, I knew it was fleeting and the thing that wasn't fleeting, that never left, was my love for you and my picture of you and me and nothing else, and that was stronger than the white lines of More but they were there and with just a little more time, I could make Hoyle what he wanted, and I had grams and grams and grams of that more time, stashed in baggies ready for the pickup.

It wasn't a vague sense of euphoria, false confidence or a general feeling of well-being. No, it was what God's own heart felt like the moment he said, "Let there be light" and the center of the universe that wasn't there exploded and time and space scattered and splattered in all dimensions and Everything began in an instant, the first instant of infinite instants to come. Someone might laugh at the thought of empathizing with God, but I did, I really did. Every moment I'd ever felt a love of anything was coursing through me a million moments a second, independent of the associated memories that spawned them, just the love and happiness untethered, unchecked, ballooning bigger than my chest would hold but they kept expanding, like my heart was the center of the big bang and I was God and more love of everything was going to blow 360 degrees in every dimension.

I wasn't afraid of White. He was under the gun from Hoyle, and who was to say what board of directors Hoyle reported to? His corner office, high-back chair and hand-carved humidor came at a price. This would be over soon, but for the moment I just wanted to bathe in the heat and feel the love move through me.

I came down and I thought I would take a shower and then I wouldn't have to do any more, but the need was bigger than the fear of Toe Tag or Manhattan White and the Bug Men that were certain to come swarming from the black desert sky.

My prostate turned into a smoking cinder, like someone had shoved a fireplace poker up my ass and I still couldn't stop yet all I could think of with each load spilled into the dirt was how much I loved you, and it shot through me like a wave of everything in the universe becoming everything else, even if I couldn't seem to hold a thought together. Desiree, I never thought it would go that far and I never thought I could go farther than that with you or White. What, were you seeing him, too?

I had to slow down, slow down, keep the head together. I was trying to think of a fallback plan. Okay, we couldn't replicate the stuff, we simply couldn't. I'd made a bunch of good LSD, and I meant solid, and some good X. In truth, I was smart, rationing some from each batch for just such an emergency, knowing that I was doing right if I met quota, kept up with production and made them money, even if it meant sand-bagging numbers at the end of every month at the extreme risk of pissing off White if he found out, but I was their goose, their golden goose, and what was good for me was good for the gander and what was a gander, anyway?

So, I had a big batch all set aside, so I had a backup plan. I could tell White, "Hey, no luck on the shit, but you know what? We've got about half a million in high-grade LSD, absolutely clean and I just know we can move it through our Carlsbad and Berkeley connections, right?" They wouldn't complain. They'd give me more time if it kept making them money, more money than they were accustomed to.

I had to think, think, think, think, think. What was good for the goose was good for the gander and I was the goose and I could have used some chicken. I wasn't hungry but I should've eaten, and there was that diner a few hours down the road and if I could just wait for the next batch then I could call it a night and walk as long as it took because it wasn't like I was going to sleep anytime soon. I could get something to eat, and I meant I could force-feed myself if I had to, and then get back to the lab, tell White no go but not make any excuses, because as much as White hated excuses, Hoyle hated them even more and Toe Tag probably couldn't even spell "excuse" but it was still up to him to pack my empty skull with sand before he ditched me in the lake if my nonexcuse excuses weren't satisfactory to White and Hoyle.

Sometimes I envied that clumsy biker with the LSD. Ignorance was bliss, even if bliss meant smoking a hollowed out gecko full of pencil shavings in the desert and surviving on tarantula meat.

If I lost that batch then I was back to nothing, I wouldn't have anything to show for everything but I knew the batch had to go for another four hours and I couldn't stand still and I couldn't keep moving and I was going to kill whatever kept making that noise. So I did another blast.

I had stopped combing my hair days ago. If you could have seen me then, Desiree, you would have laughed. Would you remember me? I was the guy who could iron the pleats in a skirt of yours if I had to, and showed you how to use soda water and newspaper to clean glass. I was wearing the same clothes that I'd been in for days because changing clothes didn't seem to matter, and I looked at myself in the mirror and I thought, yeah, it did matter, maybe I should have shaved and spruced up and I said that I would, after just one more hit, and that was what I did and then the shit I was hitting bored a hole in the bottom of my day and the time just collapsed through the bottom like a rotting grain silo and then I woke up with a heart attack just out of my field of vision and my dick in my hand, saying, I love you I love you I love you over and over to the fucking silverfish crawling in the baseboards and that, my dear sweet love of my life, is how things were without you and I'd done everything I could to keep you from knowing that.

twenty-one

ONCE I HAD A SYSTEM, IT BECAME IMPOSSIBLE TO NOT SEE IT WORKING AND it became easier to see other systems, to see the street working, to see the shell of complicity over the machinations of street dealing and know that the Powers were beholden to Powers above them, who were in turn beholden to a row of high-back chairs on a raised dais. Hoyle was everywhere, and he got his cut or you got cut.

The problem was I started seeing systems everywhere, and the possibility of a threat was no different than the possibility of a system. I had to assume it was real.

Otto told me about a dealer who used to hang out at a bar. He was part of his own chain. Nobody else in his network knew one another, they were all there at the same time, blending in with his regulars. Every night at 7:00 he played a song on the jukebox, and that song became the code word for that night if you wanted to talk to somebody in his chain. A runner hit a string of other bars, dropping quarters into the Wurlitzers for the waiting zombies nursing tap water or cheap beer. By 8:00, everyone was dispersed, whispering into pay phones and through porno theater curtains. The street came alive with zombies trolling the corners saying "Folsom Prison Blues," "Phantom 309" or "Paranoid" under their breath, and the long-range eyes and ears, the moles packing tapeworms, could only wonder at what they were hearing and what it meant.

Another network convened in the same place every week, in the same coffee shop. They'd note the license plate of the first white car they saw that day together, and the first three digits became the code for that week, followed by the last three digits in response. They never told anyone else, and the selection was too random for anyone to intercept and decipher.

Samuel Morse reduced every letter of the alphabet into a series of dots and dashes, and anything could be a dot or a dash, a sound, a color, an object or a word.

Knowing these systems, I'd perfected them to hide my signals and cover my tracks. The signals were everywhere.

My nose burned, my mouth bitter with the faint solvent tang, and I wanted to eat but I wasn't hungry and anyway, if I tried to eat, everything would taste like ketones. A full liter of meth remained in the lab, sealed in a shatterproof lab beaker like motor oil, the clear luminous brown of an animal's eyes, zero impurities, waiting to be basified into crystal.

The word "random" has no meaning for me, and doesn't exist in the universe that I know. Flip a coin three times and you might get the same result and see no pattern. Flip it a hundred times and the pattern begins to emerge. The trick to burying a signal is to know where the patterns are around you and to hide your signal within them. It works the same way with learning to see them, the coded messages flying around that the senders and receivers think you're oblivious to, but you're not.

I kept running records of utility vehicles at the gas station down the road. I had a clear view with my binoculars of my nearest neighbors, both no closer than a mile, but I watched for plumbers and cable installers, mail carriers and gas meter readers. I checked the vehicle numbers on their 800-lines, and made notes of the mailman's routes and times. Anybody else—the plumber, courier, salesmen—I checked their listings in the phonebook. I noted on each entry when the radar detector wired to the roof went off, because if it happened enough with a certain vehicle, then the coincidence became a pattern and I saw trouble.

The reflex was already reflex at that stage, reaching for the glass pipe and the amber resin to make everything okay again, to have every fear and worry gone in a second and the rush of a preorgasm split second sustained for the duration of the night. Any sense of any double meaning that could have sent me running in fear was gone. Otto was a machine spying on me, Otto was working for Hoyle without me knowing, Otto had folded and now Toe Tag was dumping him for the catfish, none of it mattered.

I had work to finish, with only forty-eight hours left, never mind the first twenty-four were gone in a blast of lust like I'd never felt before, like a marathon blow job during a skydive freefall, and I had to focus on the next. The dog kept piping up, barking and yipping at phantom intruders, nearby raccoons or coyotes. I ignored him, tried to pour through my notes, but could only think of you Desiree, and all the things I wanted to do to you.

I wrote the words "nobody ever comes" on the bathroom mirror with a bar of soap. I knew the truth, every footstep, rooftop thump, distant car was at best a brain misfire. Every time, nobody pounded on the door, no matter how long I was braced for it. If I heard it, I'd listen closely for the sound again but it never repeated itself. Peeking through the blinds or pressing my ear against the door only encouraged the delusion. Nobody ever comes, and I had to keep reminding myself of that. Stop letting my eyes jump to whatever peripheral movement caught them; stop scratching. That was tough. If the bugs or rats or snakes crawled to the center of my vision, they were real. But don't try to force them.

I felt my skin flush with the hot waves that came from sleep deprivation, the whistling in my ears continued, unabated. I'd lost count of the misfires in the lab downstairs. I sat in the living room, a pulverized gram and a glass of desert tap water in front of me, and a lump of cotton in my nose. I'd drawn molecule after molecule, checked every possible set of notes and sat dry-docked at 98 percent of completion, and that 2 percent made all the difference in the universe. Like I'd dismantled and reassembled an engine, then discovered a shop rag full of bolts with no idea where they belonged.

I'm sitting with grease under my nails in a pair of coveralls, scratching at my head because I've got bugs crawling through my hair and I don't have the remotest idea where this here oxygen came from, or this nitrogen, it's got to be from something else. I know I'm wrong. It's pickup time tomorrow, and I'd better be there with a big pile of skin. If I'm not, the coyote will be singing at the top of his voice a map to Oz.

The crickets had a code, and I was onto them. I didn't have any way of looking up the normal cadence of the locusts chirping, but I knew it was some kind of mating call or territorial thing or some way of scaring off enemies, which was ironic given the bats were spitting silent shrieks all over the air and bouncing off each other looking for food and the stupid crickets were all but screaming "Here I Am" to the world of predators at large. Not those crickets, not that night, and maybe that's why the bats were ignoring them.

Chirp, chirp, chirp, chirp, chirp. Long, short, long, eight short, long, two short, two long, short, then silence. I'd been scratching them onto notebook paper for hours and I'd lost count in the thousands. They knew I was listening, and the pauses that indicated the dots and dashes were too short for even the bats' ears to hear and they sure as shit all sounded the same to me. The sound carried for maybe a hundred yards, passed on to the crickets at that point, and everything I was doing was relayed back to Hoyle across the desert and west to Los Angeles and I was dead. I think the owl was in on it too. I couldn't see it, but I heard it. Like a larval black helicopter, the owl didn't make a sound when it flew but it was hooting from somewhere in the dark, talking to the crickets. Hoot, hoot, hoot. Four short, seven long.

I became incapable of filtering out the excess noise from the signals. My boyhood laid the groundwork for it, having always believed in a God that watched me every time I looked at a woman or jacked off, but rewarded my good behavior with a sound beating. When you could discern a real threat from everything else, it was called caution. When you couldn't, it was called paranoia. Like someone who heard every noise at the same volume, the sounds were always there, you became crazy when you heard them all at once.

You cannot separate paranoia from knowledge. The more you know, the more possibilities you see. The more possibilities you see, the more possibilities someone else sees. The more "someones" there are, the more "they" there are. It's a matter of simple math before you realize that They might not like you.

Another hit but the syringe did nothing, and I was running low on them and I couldn't sleep and I wished I had a gun, a real, honest-to-

God, shotgun because I could hear things outside and I held still and I waited. I heard footsteps or a voice or a car tire crunching on the crushed shells in the driveway and I stopped, held my breath and listened, and all I could hear were the crickets chirping. And that was when I realized what they were doing, just as the sun had gone down and the darkness had overtaken.

So, I was outside with a can of bug spray, standing silently and listening, homing in on the chirping. The good thing about crickets is that you don't have to be quiet. They used to be scattered in fields around fortresses in China, so intruders would set them off. Locusts for an alarm. Next thing I knew, I was back inside, I'd doubled up on the hit, almost a full goddamned gram into the syringe and it was a scary thing to think about when every time anyone you knew has ever been high, it was measured in milligrams, and there I was shooting a thousand milligrams of speed straight into my bloodstream and after the Devil was done snaking his fingers around my heart and down through my chest and grabbing my balls, he was gone in a puff of nothing and in the next instant I had God's smile warming me from the inside out and I just wanted to fuck someone, anyone. I still had my head about me, and I was outside again, in the dark, with the pump can sprayer of pesticide, following the chirps in the dead of night and letting loose a blast of malathion under the darkness of the new moon until I was choking on the cloud I couldn't see in the dark and the chirping stopped. Great idea, Hoyle, good messengers, but you'd have to engineer some bugs that didn't die when you sprayed them. I had always been smarter than you, and I always would be.

Checking the place for traces of me, I set up the UV lights and started scanning. I couldn't do anything about the dog hair or shit smell. Lights off, glowing purple spot on, the first thing to jump out at me is a glowing orange dot in the corner that moved as soon as I set my eyes on it. Otto had been stoned, marking the bugs with luminescent paint and tracking them at night. I missed him and wanted to slap him both in the same instant. Then another orange dot, then a glowing green and a blue then four yellow dots behind me. The pizza crusts and candy bar wrappers and frozen dinner foil traces were enough to draw them out, and after keeping the lab clean for so long it was a gargantuan cockroach rave, all of them wearing their glow paint for their big blowout party before they're crushed beneath the heel of God's jackboot.

The bugs were coming out. These were real. I hadn't expected them again and I couldn't help but smile. Little neon green beetles, and another splotch of pink crawling along the baseboard where the walls joined the rotting carpet. I had to forget the noise in my head for a while so I killed the lights and fired up the UVs and it was like lighting a frozen frame of orange, red, green and purple sparks, a dashboard splatter of alien blood from a saucer crash. They were everywhere, a multicolored flashback to Dad's firefly pictures.

Most of them were orange, so I called them carbon. If I could make the game last long enough, forget everything else, then the black helicopters would get bored and go back to their giant, metal nests, and if I was lucky, any of them empty-handed as far as transmissions were concerned, the queen would tear their rotors off and suck their tanks dry, throw the carcasses to scrap.

Blue was a logical choice for oxygen, which left green for nitrogen, and red for hydrogen. I tossed bits of my sandwich out onto the carpet, let them sniff it out. They moved like a slow-motion rendering of a high-speed switchboard.

That assignment seemed to work, given the amount of luminous red cockroaches that seemed to be balancing the organic chains. As soon as I decided on the assignments, molecules and structures started jumping out at me, like seeing patterns in the ceiling or shapes in the clouds, it was unavoidable.

Some of them were solid amines that resembled compounds already known, others were too unstable or too unworkable with open-ended chains that couldn't be made into rings without the addition of another nitrogen atom that would throw the electron balance off and destroy the stability. Others were in plain sight, MDMA, LSD, methamphetamine, ketamine, one after the next. I watched a large red roach scurry from one end of the meth molecule to the other, chasing food or a mate I don't know which, but when it stopped it'd changed the bond completely, and when the others moved, they'd formed MDMA. As the glowing bugs converged on the crumbs, I watched the molecules coalesce into shape—water became oxygen became ammonia became aluminum. I watched a dance of alchemy that man had been trying to replicate for almost a millennium. Gold became lead became chlorine. Lead became gold became skin.

"Wait. Hold it there." Yes, I was talking to a room full of luminous, spray-painted cockroaches. "You've got it. Don't move." You had to be there.

The luminous dots had held a random configuration that wasn't random, but held discrete molecules that had the properties I was looking for. I'd thought about pressing the separate components into a single binder to buy time with Hoyle. But every possible combination had been tried in clubs and elsewhere over the years, but no effects like the ones we were hearing about had ever been reported.

The bugs though, had shown me the molecular bond that seemed so obvious in hindsight, but I hadn't been able to see it. I had to move another green cockroach beside the pair of red ones, and I knew just how to do it.

They were little atoms running around, maybe they had it, and that was when I felt the big bang again, only without a syringe because that time, I knew I'd got it. The only clean paper I had was the back of your picture I kept in my bag unless I wanted to run to the basement for a clean notebook, and I couldn't risk it. I sketched as quickly as I could, finishing the last ring before the molecule crumbled then reformed as vitamin A.

I only knew why it worked in pieces, not the whole compound, but I knew it worked. Skin only perceived three sensations, pain, pressure and temperature. The subtle interplay of those very crude sensations could create a symphony of touch that constitute all the physical contact in our lives. And the memory neurotransmitters could be blocked as a side effect or a primary process but in either case, the sense of touch was real, and if the memory neurotransmitters were being blocked, then the sensation of time passing was the same, but the memory of the time that had passed would be totally different.

The original source of the alkaloid still eluded me, but I knew I could synthesize it. The bugs had been talking to me and, for once, it was my turn to listen to them.

twenty-two

I'D RESURRECTED SKIN OUT OF THE ASHES AND GLOWING ROACHES, MY PARTING gift to Hoyle. The universe was bright again. I was finished. I could hand Hoyle the keys to a network of laboratories, all six stages removed from everything but his legend, and walk away. I'd become excess overhead and Hoyle would be happy to pay me off and see me gone. One thing I learned from the tables on the Strip, you walk away when you're hot.

I reached the pay phone at the haunted gas station, sank a pile of quarters and dialed your number.

"Hello?" You said, your voice a sleepy rasp. I hadn't thought I might be waking you.

"It's me, baby. Wake up."

"Eric? Where are you? Where's Otto?"

"Dee, let's forget Otto for a minute."

"What time is it?" Headlights flooded the phone booth. A semi passed on the highway, hauling a load of propane.

"I don't know," I said. "It's late. Listen, Dee. I'm coming back. The job is almost up."

"That's good news, sweetie." Your lips were half wedged against the pillow, the phone barely against your face.

"No, it's great news. Dee, I'm a millionaire. It's why I've been working so hard, it's all coming together."

"I don't understand. Eric, honey, can we talk about this tomorrow?"

"No, we can't. Listen to me, Dee. I need you to come get me."

"Where are you?"

"I'm outside Palmdale, off Highway 138, near Littlerock." I told you to look for the phantom gas station and hotel, next to a bus stop where nobody ever waited and no bus ever came. "I need you to come get me. Right now."

"Eric, that's two and a half hours away. That's the middle of nowhere. What are you doing there?"

"I can explain when you get here. Now…please. I need you here. Now."

"Eric, I don't know what's wrong with you, but after the last couple of weeks, you can't expect to wake me up in the middle of the night and drive halfway to Las Vegas to pick you up."

"Don't start with me, Desiree." I hit the side of the phone booth with my fist. "You've got my car, remember? My car. I'd appreciate a little gratitude. I'll take you anywhere you want, after tonight. We can drive to Vegas."

"Not Vegas again."

"We can drive to Vegas," I repeated myself, louder, "get a nice room for a night or two, maybe three, and fly anywhere you want after that."

"Eric, that sounds great. But you're still scaring me. And Otto's not here."

"I know."

"I know you know. Is that all you can say?"

"What am I supposed to say?"

"I thought he was with you."

"He was, and he ran off. He's probably coyote meat, by now."

"Jesus, Eric."

"Dee, I'm sorry. Please, drive out here. Screw your job. I can take care of everything. Me and the pooch are waiting."

"You mean you've got him?"

"Yes. I told you I had him."

"Eric," you said something, the drone of another passing truck drowned you out. "And it's not funny. You're supposed to be taking care of him."

"He's fine. He's a bundle of joy."

"No, Eric, he's not fine. You left his pills here."

"He's all better, obviously."

"Goddamn you, Eric. Stop playing with me. Stop it. Can you please just once make sense and tell me what you've done with him? He's really sick."

"What's the matter?"

"If you had his medicine you'd know. He's got a tapeworm."

twenty-three

YOUR HYSTERIA ESCALATES TO PURE SOUND, AN AIRLESS ELECTRIC ANGER stuttering like the shrill shriek of a fax machine in my ear. The film breaks, the receiver blinks from my hand back to the cradle.

New moon black sky of a cold Mojave night, legions of crickets chirping in unison, he's here, he's here, he's here, he's here, he's here, relaying my death warrant at the speed of sound. Your dog had clocked every second of my last three days. Along with seventy-two hours of footage logged in his head, he'd enjoyed unchecked access to my financial records and notes—Skin, its molecular diagram and my initial proposal of its synthesis. Your mutt planned to give me those big, innocent eyes and pine for me to take him back to Mommy, to you, and hand over my work on a fuzzy, brown-eyed platter.

I hadn't slept in four days or eaten in six, or the other way around, I couldn't be certain. The phone at the gas station was contaminated and Otto was awol, but your dog didn't know you'd given him up. I needed to eat, pull my head together and make a plan.

The light hurt, like staring into a brilliant white sun flecked with gold and dried ketchup. Hank Williams crooned from the hole in his heart. A roach darted from behind the napkin dispenser, its shadow fluttered in the corner of my eye then lay buried beneath a mound of sugar and glass shards after I'd swung at it. The waitress dropped the chrome lid of the sugar jar onto my table.

"We're not going to have a problem, are we?" She was pretty, about forty, the kind of forty the desert makes you. Reptile leather tan and a white apron, a murky rose inked onto her wrist.

"Sorry," I said. "I'm a little jumpy. I've been driving and my rig broke down and I had to walk a long way and I haven't slept."

A man sitting at the counter laughed. Cowboy boots and a trucker's gut.

"You gonna order something?"

"I'm with the circus and my rig broke down."

"Are you going to eat or are you going to leave?"

I ordered a cup of decaf and a tuna melt, made sure she saw my cash. Stuffing the roll back to my pocket, I felt the loose stash of specimens from my earlier scavenging, the Fireflies. The kid had been more greedy than cautious, and he'd parted with almost three-hundred hits which I'd split among my pockets, turning up a few stray Black Widows in the process. My carelessness would get the better of me, land me in jail or worse. Especially the Black Widows. They'd been an experiment and they'd been mean. We never made them again.

My face down, the white tabletop bleaching my eyes, I stared at the menu and each time I heard the chimes ringing against the glass doors, I counted, one thousand, two thousand, three thousand, then slowly looked up to check for cops.

Above the cash register, a stuffed and mounted elk head kept vigil over the customers, a beast like some cross between a deer, bull and moose. I'd seen them in the high desert, almost hitting one while driving through the hills of New Mexico, rounding a black bend in the dead of night with no road shoulder, no room for error, my headlights hit a pair of giant, almond eyes that lit up and hovered in the dark. Now I knew where visions of aliens came from. I could scarcely imagine the amount of surveillance hardware packed into that massive, alien elk head.

A busboy swept up the sugar and glass, replaced my silverware. Things were falling into place. Your mutt didn't know you'd given him up. He was only a threat if I served as his courier. I could eat, walk back to the house, grab my notes, retrieve my cash, wipe the place down and disappear. I'd phone White with good news from the diner payphone, rendezvous with him over a tuna melt. With my cash savings and instructions for Hoyle's product, I could say good-bye to Oz, Manhattan White, Hoyle and the Chain forever.

My food arrived. I smelled methyl chloride residue, used to decaffeinate the coffee. The diner probably held fifty or sixty pounds in their storeroom, enough trace methyl to bind to a hundred different hosts and reinvent the chemical wheel. Nudge a molecule, an atom. The difference between amphetamine and methamphetamine is both minuscule and gargantuan, and that guillotined elk head knew it, staring at me from its cedar trophy mount trying to look stupid.

Turning my back to it, I moved to the other side of the booth and dumped pepper onto my french fries but the Head stared at me in the window's reflection. Facing me made no difference. The Head didn't need to see my eyes, all it needed was the proper frequency and minimal interference. Neurotransmitters fire in a symphony code, blood rushes to lobes working in concert to form a given thought, making for cranial hot spots that show up on thermographs taken by black helicopters and stuffed elk heads. A candle is an X-ray, it's a matter of wavelength. Trying to not think about something, like pinching off a gushing hose, creates more pressure and blasts the thoughts out faster and the place smelled like shit and the lights were too bright and what I could do with all of that methyl chloride and then I got it: the Head heard me.

"I'm not doing a goddamned thing." Twisted around in the booth to look the Head square in its alien surveillance eyes just as the music stopped, so the words sounded louder than I'd intended and now everyone else was staring at me as well. We are going to have a problem. If I paid up, tipped well and left quickly, they'd have no reason to stop me or call anyone.

Forty bucks for a decaf and a tuna melt, one hand on the door and one step to safety.

"I hope that hunter shot you in the ass and killed all your children." I couldn't contain myself.

Walking back, I tried calming myself before the fear flushed fight-or-flight juices into my system, sucking the blood from my hands and feet, flaring my pupils, raising my pulse and temperature. That's what the helicopters look for, helicopters painted the color of a moonless midnight and fueled on the souls of the dead so their rotors pump the air in silence, their scopes checking for heat and they see a glowing head and torso with no arms or legs floating midair, they register panic and come after you, bugmen sliding down ropes dangling from black helicopters churning out silent hurricanes over the dirt.

A firefly blinked in the dark. *There aren't any fireflies out here.* As soon as the thought left my brain, the firefly blinked off, stayed off. I walked faster, my sweat freezing in the night air, and it came back, four of them this time, dancing at the edges of my eyes then gone.

They followed me from the diner. They were doing panic recon. The crickets tipped them off. I stood still, cleared my head, starting at the top of the list: television jingles, sitcom one-liners and grade school jokes to bury the blood-symphony of thought giving them nothing to hear but a false alarm.

A tentative step, then a second, then a third until a firefly blinked on again. The worst kind of firefly, the alpha, the quivering red sniper dot. It landed dead-center on my heart, smoke curling from my jacket as it burned through. Another blinked on, then another, my chest and arms lighting up with angry red pinpoints, metropolitan Hell seen from a burning airplane. The glowing bugs covered me, their hot feet grazing my cold skin as they swarmed to my kill zones, a thousand of them for the thousand snipers a thousand miles away with their night vision scopes trained on my head and chest, awaiting the signal to leave my steaming corpse for the coyotes.

"Pull your goddamned triggers already."

Nothing. The fireflies gone in a blink. My jacket was cool to my touch in the night air. A cricket chirped, a coyote howled. I measured their sounds for a discernible code but heard none, so continued back to Oz.

The clock read 3:30 A.M. I remembered something about food and a head with enormous glowing eyes. I'd been abducted. The aliens fed me a tuna melt.

Your dog stared at me from the floor, his pink tongue hanging out of his little salon-groomed, rodent face. He wanted me to pick him up. He wanted to lick me. He wanted a DNA sample from my face.

"No go," I said. "Mommy Machine sold you out. She must be a prototype because they're not supposed to fall in love." He didn't get it, he just worked those pathetic, cartoon baby seal eyes and twitched his tail. "Are you listening? I know who you are. Mommy caved and told me everything. Mommy's going to be shut down and sold for scrap."

My diagram was tacked to the wall, a black marker map of a tryptamine molecule with my insect-inspired brainstorm written below. A green nitrogen roach tapped at its corner. I flicked it and tucked the drawing into my pocket.

"I wish you hadn't seen this," I said. "I've got no problem with you. I'm not gonna hurt you, but I'm not taking you with me. Mommy knows where we are and she'll come for you. You can tell her whatever you want, once I'm long gone."

Fuzzface barked. I filled four bowls with water, covered the kitchen floor with newspaper, sliced open the fifty-pound bag of dog food and dumped it on its side, then checked all of the locks, unplugged the fax machine and police scanners. I didn't need them anymore. I changed into a clean shirt then emptied my overnight bag, heading down to the basement to make my last withdrawal.

The projector keeps skipping. It might be my memory, it might not.

My hands shook and I couldn't hold the numbers in my head. The hairline gap around the edge of the tumbler hissed like a punctured tire. The numbers, six, two, one, crowded each other out of the scant space left in my brain. I couldn't form pairs and, once I could, I dialed the same six-digit sequence in the same direction, right, right, right. The dog licked my arms and yelped, the sound hitting my eardrums like a knitting needle and when I stomped down on the safe door out of sheer frustration, he ran for cover and left me alone.

If I could shut my eyes for an hour, I could pull it together. I had everything I needed to walk away and give Hoyle what he wanted, but I wasn't leaving behind $630,000 in the safe simply because I was too wired to remember the combination. Leaving. Left. Left. Left. Right, left, right.

A quick bump and all was right with the world. Right, left, right. The tumbler hummed, the handle gave and I heaved the door open, laughing with relief. A candy bar wrapper, a ballpoint pen and a lone AA battery lay inside the safe. Bundled Jacksons, sequentially serialized, face up, in blocks of a thousand, fifty each—$630,000 altogether gone.

Along with my stomach and pulse. Nobody but Otto and I knew a safe existed in the lab. Nobody but Otto and I knew the numbers for it.

You and your dog had been clocking me from day one, Desiree. You read my mind, used your cards to know every move I made before I made it, didn't you? Your dog fed you everything else you needed to know and now Otto had jumped ship with everything I'd saved. Otto, stay far away from here because when I call White and ask for Toe Tag myself, I'll know exactly what I'm doing.

Thunder outside. The universe decided to rain now that I had to walk until sunrise. The house shook from another rumble and your dog yelped and whined, scared out of his wits, afraid of shorting out and smoking his circuits if the lightning came too close. Me, I could dance on the rooftops with a golf club. The wrath of the angels hit me when I was younger, so they couldn't touch me a second time.

They weren't giving up, though. The thunder clapped louder and Oz trembled under the boot heels of more angry angels like those who'd chased Dad and me into the cellar when I was a boy, only this one kept shouting my name. I heard it a second time, my name muffled by the storm. Your dog circled my feet, whining. More thunder, then my name again. The gas station phone was crawling with tapeworms, the diner was monitored by the Head who'd signaled the helicopters who'd followed me back to Oz. They were outside. No mistaking it. No mistaking the sound of my name and the meaty end of an angry fist hammering against the door, shaking the windows.

I was too far panicked for more. The next threshold would either be death because my heart or some vessel in my brain exploded or a Zen priest's calm that preceded some rash, violent flip of a self-destruct switch.

The surveillance dog kept barking, louder and louder, hot puffs of electric dog breath like smoke signals in the cold air, calling them down to the basement. They'd catch me while I stood helpless and staring at the fading string of air barks from the spy dog. If he saw me leave, he'd tell them where I went, and he'd bark it out in that TV dog bark code. Code. The pulses dissolved midair, the chain never longer than four or five at once, but that was enough. Bark, bark, bark, bark. Long, short, long, long and indeed, I was calm, as tranquil as deep space and just as clear:

The basement lab had a full pound of pharmaceutical-grade MDMA, unpressed and uncut, and twelve pounds of methamphetamine in various stages of recrystallization, together worth over $150,000.

I shut off the cooling.

The six, uncut blotter sheets of LSD had a wholesale value of more than $36,000 for more than five-thousand individual hits.

I opened each of the eight five-gallon drums of ether. The dog would stop barking any second.

Three hundred Mad Hatters awaited pickup, along with an equal amount of White Rabbits and Mr. Toads, as well as a hundred Yellow Submarines and Blue Meanies. Their combined street value came to $28,000. The lab gear was worth just under $75,000.

The barking stopped.

I cut the power.

I had an open gallon of toluene and a one percent chance of not being shot when I opened the cellar door. A quick peek through the cracks and I opened the door slowly—no sparks—and stepped out into the night and my one percent of luck. I dumped the toluene behind me, let it cascade down the steps to the pooling ether fumes below. Your photograph was in my pocket. I kissed your picture once, lit the corner and dropped it onto the concrete stairs. That picture of your face saved me, for a little while.

I ran. Between the flash and the roar, there wasn't any space at all. The desert lit up daylight for four seconds and I ran as fast I could for each one. Every night creature imaginable was all at once exposed beneath the screaming light of the burning houses: coyotes, prairie dogs, spiders the size of my open hands and rattlesnakes like ropes of liquid muscle. Without the light from Oz, I would have died.

The fire lulled and a wave of darkness followed that lasted for no more than a few moments. I slowed my run and when the second blast sounded, a hot wind bent the sage and the desert shrubs to the ground. Stopping to breathe, I looked back. A ball of fire, half the size of the house itself, rose to the sky. Beautiful.

The desert life burrowed from the apocalypse, and the massive fireball dispersed into angry tongues of flame scattering in every direction and then, in a whirlwind motion, they came back together. The bats were on fire, they were pissed and looking for me. I had to outrun my own echo.

I ran until the fire was too far behind me to light my way, and then walked in the dark, ducking off the road when I saw headlights. Fatigue pulled at my feet, the sluggish quicksand of delirium wrapped around my chest and neck, choking me. A distant streetlight shone over the highway intersection, the abandoned gas station from where I'd called you earlier. The line was contaminated, but I had no other option. As I felt my pockets for change, the tablets I'd been carrying at the diner turned up again, the only incriminating evidence left. Lab or not, they were enough to send me to jail. I should have thrown them away but I couldn't think clearly. I panicked and swallowed them.

That's right about where my memory gets fuzzy.

twenty-four

My memory bites its own tail amid the flaming bats and melting nails as Oz implodes into a smouldering bruise in the desert. The distant flames die down and the phone booth goes dark. I can't see anything except the black metal and plastic of the phone itself, though I don't remember it having a green light. My eyes adjust, and I'm not in the phone booth. The green light is from the coin box of booth number four and, in the dark, I feel the wood from the guillotine panel protecting the Glass Stripper from the world outside her pink room.

Either I'm dropping through the floor, or the coin box is floating away. I reach for it, catching a light switch and the overhead bulb washes out the glow from the black light, and a painted green roach scurries down the wall, behind my bed.

I blink, and my life is over.

I'm sober, though I can't say I'm clearheaded. Morrel meets me at the courthouse and gives me a sport jacket, dress shirt and tie, and I change clothes in the bathroom. Morrel says I look like death, and he's right. After I change, we go across the street to a lunch counter where I drink a pot of coffee and Morrel flags the waitress and says something I can't hear. She returns with two jalapeno peppers on a saucer.

"Eat these," says Morrel.

"You're joking."

"No, I'm not. Just one, you can do it in two bites."

After the first bite, my face flushes with heat, sweat runs from my forehead and my nose feels like it's bleeding.

"What was that for?"

"You need to get some color in your face." He takes a travel pack of aspirin from his pocket and slaps it in front of me. "Take a couple of those and finish your coffee. We need to go."

My trial proceeds. Morrel and the prosecutor approach the bench, resume positions, argue over a display of evidence tagged and spread across two end-to-end cafeteria tables near the bailiff's desk like the recovered traces of an airline crash. They dispute the admissibility of each and every vial, bag, envelope, soil sample, glass shard, tire track cast, my vehicle registration and nearby phone booth records. The list seems infinite, though the court can't produce a single witness identifying me at the scene. They have no record or witness of a transaction into, or out of, the lab. Each piece of evidence is a scorched fragment of something larger and more incriminating, but on its own is shaky and open to disputes which Morrel, much to my shock, conjures out of thin air: Each exhibit's discovery location and loose proximity to the lab, fire department testimony as to the indeterminate strength of the blast and how far it could have sent certain fragments, the quantifiable, vaporizing heat at ground zero. Morrel recites a litany of raids and arrests in the surrounding area, all of which could have led to discarded or abandoned evidence. The pieces are nothing individually, but collectively they tell me what I already know. The proof of arson is absolute but, beyond that, it's a line-item fight for enough evidence to prove the rest.

I scan the courtroom for signs of anyone I recognize, hoping for you. Anslinger is nowhere to be seen, though if he's going to testify, he won't be present during the other proceedings. Manhattan White and Toe Tag, I suspect, will observe, but they're not here yet. Sometimes I look over my shoulder as the courtroom doors swing shut, and someone has either just sat down or just walked out but I never catch anyone in between. It's startling how many familiar faces I've amassed in my short time starting from nothing. The courtroom feels lonely without them. Perhaps I'll invite the Glass Stripper to come by and sit in for an afternoon when she's not working.

"Desiree," says the prosecutor.

I've completely tuned out at this point. I'm about to ask for a bathroom break, but forget it the instant I hear your name. I look behind me, hoping for your flaming hair among the spectators, but you're not there, nor are the doors swinging in your wake. My heart pounds with a mixture of hope and horror but everything's stalled. The prosecutor confers with his aide, scanning a sheet of paper and looking at a small evidence pouch.

"Your Honor," Morrell steps to the podium and addresses the judge, "the defense moves to have the exhibit stricken from the proceedings."

"These specimens were gathered by the same team, from the same burn site as part of the same investigation," says the prosecutor.

He holds up a small, glassine envelope with a property sticker affixed to one side. I could spot them from a thousand miles away: the shiny blue tablets, the reigning media scourge that brought me back into your arms at the Firebird. Their connection to me is tenuous at best, but this man plans on making his career by putting me away, the mastermind behind the latest drug scare.

"We don't see why these should be exempt," he says.

"Counselor?" The judge removes his glasses to address Morrel.

"Your Honor," Morrel begins, "if the prosecution wishes to accuse my client of any wrongdoing, especially with respect to the illegal manufacture of drugs, then the prosecution should be able to correctly identify," Morrel stresses *correctly identify* as he holds aloft a photocopied sheet, "beyond urban slang or street lingo, the illegal substance that my client is being accused of manufacturing." The prosecutor stands to speak but Morrel doesn't pause. "If you can show me court records that document a conviction of possession of 'reefer,' or 'doobie,' I'll reconsider." The courtroom chuckles, everyone but me.

"Your Honor," the prosecutor jumps at the opening. Morrel tries to stop him again but the judge silences him. "The presence of this drug is well-known and documented, as is its very recent entry into the black market. It is a new analogue without any known medical production." Once more, Morrel tries to interrupt but the prosecutor continues with his voice raised. "The speculation that it came from a pharmaceutical manufacturer is still speculation. Your Honor, whether or not the drug has an origin in a legitimate source, the fact remains that all available evidence points to it being a purely black market product. The state has nothing but its street terms with which to identify it." He produces a photocopied sheet. From a distance, it looks to be identical to the one Morrell is using. "Skin," says the prosecutor. He dons his glasses and begins reading a litany of street terms—I already know them— "Touch, Cradle, Derma, D," until Morrel cuts him short.

"The prosecution is using a girl's name, Your Honor." The courtroom breaks into laughter. "They haven't even begun to identify the substance, so it stands to reason they're not prepared to levy a charge of manufacture for something they can't identify. I will not have a client be charged with making 'Peggy Sue' in a laboratory." The courtroom bursts into outright hysterics. The judge beats the laughter into submission with his gavel, then calls the opposing attorneys to his bench, yet again.

Several minutes of mumbling and gesturing follow, a ball of lead forming in my stomach and growing heavier by the second. Morrel returns and the judge adjourns until the following day while he considers the issue at hand.

"You know anything about this?" Morrel whispers to me.

"About what?"

"The street names. Apparently it's hip to call it by a woman's name."

"It sounds familiar. You know how it is with me."

"I do. At least we know what 'Desiree' means."

I don't hear anything else. The ball of lead is falling into a gorge at terminal velocity, taking me with it, and I grip the edge of the table to keep from being pulled into the black hole below the courtroom carpet.

"Things are looking up," says Morrel. "They've got a scary mountain of evidence, but the pieces break easily. We just need to chip away at them." This is good news, I know. I'm facing a lifetime trafficking conviction and the court-appointed lawyer is showing optimism, but I don't feel it. "Loosen up, Eric. Remember, you're not even on trial, yet. We're still arguing evidence. Be here bright and early."

I've sweated through my dress shirt by the time I arrive at the theater. My head is screaming. Court adjourned around 4:00, and I haven't seen this much sunlight since ever, as far as I know. I remember seeing sunlight before the fire, but I can't trust those memories anymore. It's a long shot the Glass Stripper is working right now, but I can't bear the thought of my room. The allure of Skin is gone. I don't want to remember anymore because my memories keep getting worse.

I step into booth number four with a handful of tokens. I don't ask for Desiree this time. The Token Man assumed nothing, so extracted no toll and gave me my full change. I slide the latch shut with my bare fingers, dropping a few of the brass tokens in the dark as I'm fumbling for the coin box. The looking-glass guillotine slides up. The Glass Stripper faces away from me, entertaining someone in a window on the opposite side of the pink room. I recognize her ass. I knock on the glass once, then again harder, not caring whether or not the mop man has been slacking. She doesn't hear me. When the guillotine window opposite mine drops, I hammer the glass with my fist. She spins quickly and scowls at my window, her dancing booth charm turned to ice.

"I'm sorry." I want her to hear me, but I hate raising my voice. I slide three Jacksons through the tip slot. "I'm cool. I didn't mean to scare you."

"You didn't scare me." She takes my money, tucks it into the front of her panties. "Want a dance?"

"No."

"Good." She starts to walk away and I tap the glass again.

"Wait, can I just talk to you for a sec?"

"I have customers. You want to talk, then get a number out of a newspaper."

"I just gave you sixty dollars."

She rolls her eyes, crouches down so her face is almost level with mine. "Go."

"Do you recognize me?

"You're the guy with the booth tokens and the chafed cock, right?"

"Yeah, I mean no, not really. You might have me confused with somebody else.

"I was joking," she says. She hasn't stripped yet, but what little she's wearing I could ball up into my fist. More sleight of hand, she pulls a cigarette and a lighter out of thin air. She lights up with a deep drag, but says nothing else.

"Desiree, please. Just look at me. Have we ever met before, outside of this place?"

"I'm not Desiree." She blows a cloud of smoke against the glass.

"I know. Your name isn't Desiree. It's a stage name. I won't ask your real name."

"Yes, you won't ask my real name and no, you don't know my stage name. My name is Charlene on the dance roster. And that's the only name you'll get from me."

"No, I asked for Desiree. He sent me to you." I jut my thumb behind me, back where the Token Man sits outside the booth doors.

"Of course he did. And yes, of course I recognize you."

Good. She understands me, at least.

"So you know I'm cool." I'm calmer now, and I speak in a whisper. "And your name is Desiree, right?"

The booth flashes blue with the noise of a cracking whip and my nose burns with electricity. I was staring at her eyes or following the glowing cigarette tip, I don't know, but I was right up against the window trying to whisper to her when this sleight-of-stripper had one hand free and out of sight, and now she's poking the chrome teeth of a stun gun through the tip slot, right against my belly after the warning snap that sent me all the way back to a smoking pear tree that might or might not have ever existed.

"Don't move," she says. "Who sent you?"

There's no move I can make that's faster than her squeeze of the trigger. Out of reflex, my hands are in the air and a cascade of brass coins hits the floor of the booth, a sound I know with more certainty than anything I've felt without a brain load of Skin.

"Some guys from my hotel," I tell her. "They said to ask for you."

"You mean Desiree."

"Yeah. Desiree." The one thing worse than being wrong is being uncertain.

"What hotel?"

"The Firebird." Strange, I haven't told anyone where I've been until this moment. "It's about a half mile from here."

"I know where it is."

"A couple of guys who live there. Jack. He's got a friend. A skinny guy who doesn't talk."

"I know them."

"So you know his friend's name?"

"No." Then she whispers, "And you cleaned me out last time."

"Who's your supplier?"

"Not a chance," she says, and stands to leave.

"Wait, please. Who is Desiree?" I need to hear it, I need to know for certain.

"Nobody. It's code. You should know that."

"Code for what?"

Her eyes freeze, glassy like the camera eyes of the elk head. She grinds her cigarette out with her stiletto toe. The edge of the pink carpet by my window is burned and blackened with dead cigarette butts.

"I'm clean," I tell her. "I'm not setting you up," and I loosen my tie, start to unbutton my shirt but she shakes her head, waves her hands at me to stop.

"You have to go now."

I button my shirt, then ask her, "Can you read palms?"

She says nothing, but mouths the word "go" at the glass.

"I know it's a strange question. But do you read palms? Or can you tell someone's fortune with cards? Yes or no."

Another lightning blast flares in the booth. She's holding the miniature cattle prod at her own waist level, behind the glass where it can't possibly touch me but the sight and sound of the microlightning still threatens to burst my heart open.

"No," she says. "Now get out."

"Just tell me again, your name isn't Desiree. Your real name. I don't care what it is, as long as you tell me it's not Desiree."

If she says anything, I don't hear it. My time runs out and the guillotine window drops, shutting out the pink light for the last time. As soon as I step from booth number four, the Token Man has one hand around the back of my neck and the other around my wrist, twisting my arm behind me and I go limp with fear, feeling my healing burns stretched to near ripping at the edges. I land on the sidewalk. A mailbox stops my tumble into the street.

twenty-five

I NEED TO FORGET EVERYTHING ALL OVER AGAIN. THE STASH OF SKIN BACK IN my room could have me time-traveling inside my skull for weeks, but I want it nowhere near me. There is a very real possibility that every second I've reconstructed has been a prolonged and vivid dream, but a dream nonetheless. There is a very real possibility that I was, in fact, alone at the lab from the very beginning, that Skin was my brainchild and if I wanted to sell out everyone I ever came into contact with, I couldn't because there was no everyone. There is an equally real possibility that I was standing too close when Oz blew, though I had nothing to do with it myself. That Anslinger simply collected the evidence, found the name attached to the Galaxie and decided whoever I was, I would become Eric Ashworth, is not out of the question. I could have been in a car wreck on the way back from church, or taken a stray brick to the head on a construction site, and it's my own bad luck that I have no memory, insurance or next of kin, my own bad luck that Anslinger has a high-profile case he needs sewn shut, water-tight. That White and Anslinger know each other is not unlikely. Anything is possible and nothing is possible. They're the same thing.

Lou hasn't moved. He's behind the bar wiping a glass, the same one for all I know. Like the Glass Stripper never leaves her pink room and Jack and the Beanstalk never venture forth from the Firebird, Lou stands in the same spot, with the same expression, polishing the same glass with the same towel, each time I enter the bar. The universe is stuck and I'm the monkey wrench in God's gears. Lou asks if I'm having the usual and I say yeah, but hold the Coke.

"Throw in a Scotch and soda." Manhattan White takes the barstool beside mine, opens his wallet.

"And a Scotch and soda." I wave his money away. "No, I got it." The closest to feeling anything good today is not feeling either horror or hatred in the presence of White.

"Mind if I join you?" he asks.

"Yes."

"Do I see a glimmer of recognition?" He smiles, punching me on the shoulder like a Little League coach. I nod. More than a glimmer.

"You here to snuff me," Lou sets our drinks down and I take a stiff swallow of whiskey. "Now's your chance. You won't get a fight out of me."

"Let's not get ahead of ourselves here." White smiles. He doesn't touch his drink. "First things first. How are you doing? You get your brain plugged back in or do we need to do the whole song and dance from the beginning?" I'm having a bad day, and his jocular attitude is making it worse. "We had ice cream a few days ago, remember?"

"I remember," I say. "And before that I met you at a house out near Littlerock, off Highway 138. And I called you for help another time because somebody got hurt and that somebody disappeared."

"This is good news."

"No, it's not."

"It sounds as though your memory's returned," he says. "You got hit on the head but you're all better now."

"I was not hit on the head. I overdosed. I was brain dead for eight seconds."

"Your mind seems pretty clear to me."

"That's a relief, assuming what I remember about you is correct, because everything else is a blank. I thought my memory was coming back but I was wrong."

"Then it's none of my concern, your other business. My immediate concern is our compensation, and that you relinquish the intellectual property we spoke of last week."

"I can't help you." I drain my glass and ask Lou for a refill.

"Wrong answer. You owe us money and a chemistry lesson. Or you have a play date with my son."

"The chemistry lesson you're looking for was lost in those eight seconds." I can see pieces of the model in my mind, pieces that could as easily belong to a vitamin or a molecule of plastic, as likely as anything else. "If you're looking for a sample, I can provide it."

"We've got samples. That's not the problem."

"Then there is no problem. You have someone break it down, isolate and analyze the active alkaloid, then do a reverse synthesis. Someone with the time and equipment. I'd love to help but my laboratory's in a billion tiny pieces sealed up in an evidence locker and I seem to have forgotten my higher education while undergoing CPR."

"'Someone.' Like we put an ad in the paper for this someone?"

"Sure. Qualifications include an extensive background in organic chemistry as well as large-scale production and operations. Must have no brain damage or life-threatening enemies. Accused felons need not apply."

White laughs, as though he's genuinely enjoying my company.

"You're irreplaceable, Eric," he says. "Among the things you forgot was just how unique you were. You could have cured cancer but, lucky for us, we found you first. I'm going to miss you. Never thought I'd say that."

"Get it over with."

"Would you slow it down? You're really paranoid."

"You have no idea."

"What about the money?" White asks.

"What about it?"

"The money to cover the damage you caused. This will allow us to hire your mysterious someone."

"There is no money."

White says nothing, his face blank, waiting for me to continue, to fill in the rest.

"There's no punch line either. I've got some cash and some science projects back in my room. You're welcome to them."

"Don't force my hand, Eric. The joke's over."

"It never began. The money is gone. All of it."

White helps himself to a cocktail napkin, removes a pen from his pocket and slides them both to me.

"Jot the account number down," he says. "Right here. Write it down, I'll cover your bar tab and room rent for the rest of the month and you'll never see me again."

"The money was at the house." Everything's quiet. "Now you get it. It's gone."

"It's burned." White says.

"It was in a floor safe."

"The Feds seized it."

"Otto seized it."

"One more time." He forces a smile, like a car salesman who's been kicked in the shin.

"Otto," I repeat. "He introduced us, remember? The gambling freak. He's been skimming from the beginning. If I were you, I'd recount every bag he ever dropped off to you. He vanished a couple of weeks before the fire. Got to Oz first and cleaned me out. Haven't seen him since. You find him, your boy can be my guest, and make sure to give him my regards."

"I have business to take care of." White slips his pen back into his pocket and stands. "Let's reconvene in three days, right here. Same time. You've had your fun. I realize it might take time, but I trust you'll be carrying a very large canvas bag when we next meet."

I'm deciding on some flavor of "you haven't been listening to me," or "you must be more brain damaged than I am," but White stops me.

"Don't. I've lost my sense of humor about this. Good afternoon, Eric."

I finish my drink, then dial Anslinger. It's after hours, so I'm once more dumped to his voice mail.

"For what it's worth," I tell him, "I was left holding the bag. I had a partner, Otto, who let me take the fall. I don't know his last name. But he was there for everything, right up until he ripped me off and jumped ship. I doubt that's helpful to you right now, and I know it's too late as far as my case is concerned. But if you ever get your hands on him, I'll say or sign anything you want, if it will help you to bury him."

twenty-six

LIKE WAKING UP SICK FROM A DRUNKEN FEVER, WEARING CLOTHES YOU don't recognize and a stranger's blood on your shirt, the chaos follows a trail you don't remember leaving, right to your feet. I step into my room and it's putrid, my own stink out-stinking that of the previous occupants. The acrid smell of boric acid hangs in the air, mixing with the chemical sweat print from my body on the bed like a burial cloth, the smell sealed inside by the paper stuffed into window cracks and the steel wool in the baseboards. My collage, cardboard box flaps and pieces of torn paper, covers my walls, a floor-to-ceiling display of dead and dissected roaches, diagrams labeled with bits of string pointing to theoretical placement of tracking chips, signal boosters and recording devices. The *Blattella transmitus*. It made sense at the time.

I was wrong about the bugs, but not about being followed. Someone powerful saw to it that my bail was too low and too easy to make for the charges against me. Someone saw to it that the roll of cash I'd been arrested with was returned. It should have been seized, skimmed down to a quarter of the real amount and then booked as evidence, but they handed back every last dollar. Neither White nor Anslinger have that much pull, but Hoyle does. I need to get out of here, and they know that. When anyone refers to they, they're referring to Hoyle, whether they know it or not.

On my way in, a couple of new guys in the lobby asked where the rehab group was meeting. Big guys with muscles and work boots claiming they'd hit bottom, that the court had ordered them into a program. Either one of them was healthier than a whole floor of Firebird residents. Then another guy came to check the plumbing. He was running back and forth to his van but his hands weren't dirty and his clothes weren't wet. He was lugging a pipe wrench without fixing anything. The wrench was pristine, without a trace of lime or rust, an underused prop collecting dust in storage.

The warden seemed too friendly.

"Hey," he'd said. "Guy dropped this off for you." He handed me a white envelope with my name typed on the outside. My hands were shaking but I took it, then ran to my room before the plumber could follow me.

The whisper says, "jump," only louder this time and when I hear it again, it's no longer whispering. I step away from the window, pull the cards from the desk and spread a game in front of me. On cue, there's a knock at the door but I'm not startled this time. I know that knock.

"Nice of you gentlemen to drop by."

Jack and the Beanstalk step into my room once more, as though someone's waiting to take their hats and offer them a brandy.

"Good afternoon, sir," says Jack, spooky cordial. "It's a change to see you so engaged. I take it from your wardrobe that your trial has begun."

My trial has begun in the same sense an airplane has begun flying toward a mountain.

"And it's not going well, I gather."

"Jack, I'm not up for it today. What do you want? Or are you just here to say that you warned me?"

"I'd say you've been salting your own wounds quite well, on your own."

"Something like that."

Beanstalk examines my diagrams and dissections, writing down his observations on my elusive species in his black notebook, his headphones clamped to his ears.

"How much longer do you have left?"

"I don't know. It could be tomorrow or a week. They're still arguing the admissibility of evidence. There's a lot of it."

"And you have no disposition on the outcome?" Jack cocks his head, like someone placating a wounded child.

"I don't know what you mean."

"Are you guilty?"

Straight away, I know Jack's looking for me to spill while Beanstalk digs for evidence. Hoyle needs to know what I know. Hoyle had me cut loose. Hoyle sent me to the same hotel where Jack and the Beanstalk live who, in turn, introduced me to the Glass Stripper, who gave me back my memory.

In the next instant, my house-of-cards conspiracy theory collapses beneath a feather of doubt, and I know I'm wrong.

"I'm clean, if that's what you're wondering," Jack says. "I can show you."

"That's not it. It doesn't matter now anyway," I say. Then the words leave my mouth, "Yes, I'm guilty." No weight lifts from my shoulders, I feel no sense of relief. It's as though I'd confessed to murdering Snow White. "I thought I remembered all of the things that made me guilty, but I don't."

"Desiree isn't always reliable, that way."

"Please," I say, holding my hand up to stop Jack from saying anything else. Until the reality sinks in on its own, I want to savor the bliss of your illusion for as long as I can.

"I did projects with my dad when I was younger." I sit down on the edge of my bed and piece together what I think I know. "I learned about the way the universe works because of him. But he and my mom taught me to believe in God and those things didn't…" I'm not sure how to continue, not sure whether the Mom and Dad I remember ever existed. The white envelope from the warden sits on my bed. I'd forgotten about it, so I pick it up and I tear it open while I talk to Jack. "What I learned about God and what I learned about science didn't match. I figured out that the one place where the two ideas touch is in chemistry, in the brain."

"So, now we know what you're on trial for."

"Right. I guess you do. Only now I don't even know if I'm remembering my reasons, whether I did anything at all with my father. I think he died when I was young, but I can't be certain. I think I was hit by lightning, but I don't know." I'm talking to a polite, well-spoken junkie covered in festering sores and who talks like the killer computer from that space movie, and his semiopaque, walking stick, mute, jazz-fiend friend. "Why am I telling you all of this?"

"I already told you. The two of us," he gestures to Beanstalk with his outstretched arm and upturned palm, like he's a museum guide, "we're the only friends you've got."

I unfold the note, expecting a veiled threat composed of cut-out magazine letters, but instead find a message written in perfect block capitals:

Recovered near the burn site. Maybe it will help. Coyotes at the rest.
    –N. Anslinger

There's a second sheet behind the note. It's a photocopy of a dog collar, the page rubber-stamped as evidence and marked with my case number. It's dark and blurry, its details lost in the bloated shadows of a second-generation copy, but the tag is crisp and unblemished. It's a medallion the size of a watch face and it reads, OTTO.

"I really have hit bottom, then," I say.

"Please. That's uncalled for."

"I'm sorry." I'm starting to believe him, about the two of them being my only friends. "I never questioned the accusations. I just tried to remember what I did to bring those charges on, instead of whether or not I actually did them. And I thought maybe, just maybe, I had an idea why. I'm not a bad person. I wasn't after the money.

"But you still believe you're guilty?"

"Yes. But everything I remembered is wrong. Everything leading up to my arrival here never happened. You said I was in love. You were right. But that never happened, either."

"I know," Jack says. "Desiree. It's like falling in love every night and having your heart broken every morning. Forever, like Prometheus. Only everyone forgets how seldom our memory is accurate. Having more memory is just a way of distorting a greater amount of the past." Jack pauses, looks at his feet, and for a moment the only sound is Beanstalk scribbling into his notebook. "I'm preaching. I apologize. This isn't the time or place."

"Forget it."

"Is there anything I can do?"

"Get me out of here." I'm joking and serious at the same time.

"You can't leave on your own?"

"They're watching me. I'm a flight risk."

Jack's face is blank.

"You can believe me or not," I say.

"Suppose we believe you? Where would you go?"

I hadn't given it any thought, but the answer leaps to mind in a blink. "Back to the lab," I tell him. "Oz. What's left of it."

"You know where it is? For certain?"

"Positive. They gave the location at the trial."

"And why go there?"

"Just to see if it's like I remember it. To see if there's one thing I can recall correctly."

"So then, go."

"I can't skip out on my trial. I'll make things worse."

"They can be worse?"

Jack is not only right, but on my side for certain, this time.

"I'd just like to see the place for myself," I tell him. "Just to know I've got some details right."

"You've explained that. And I've already said it: Go."

"I can't. They're watching me. I know it."

"We'll help you."

"Why?"

"Does it matter?"

"Yes."

"Let me ask you," Jack folds his hands behind him, the learned professor. "If you believe that everything you know of your life never happened, and you could verify at least one event, one place or detail to prove at least some small part of your memory was right, would you care at all about how you did it, or who wanted to help you or stop you?"

Anything to find you, Desiree.

"No."

"Simple, isn't it? Now gather your things and follow us."

I haven't touched my supply of painkillers from the doctor and, though I scarcely remember my final buy from the Glass Stripper, I'm still holding a formidable stash of Skin, the very last of it, by her account. I stuff them all into my pockets, along with what cash I've kept in my room, which I'd hidden behind one of my bug diagrams. I had the common sense to know that a thief wouldn't be digging through those in my absence.

Beanstalk removes his headphones, presses his ear to the wall and a look of utter bliss comes over him, soothed by the same humming wires Jack had warned me against. He raises his hand and counts down with his fingers, five, four, three, two, one. The phone rings.

"Go ahead," says Jack.

I pick up the receiver. "Go." Old habit. I think.

"Uh, Mr. Ashworth"—it's the warden—"I'm wondering if it's possible to move you to another room. We've finally got an exterminator to take a look at the place."

So, now I'm getting five-star courtesy at a cash-only dump. They think I'm stupid. I repeat the question, as though to make sure I heard him correctly. When Jack and the Beanstalk hear me, Beanstalk points to his wrist, then holds up one finger.

"No problem. Can you give me an hour?"

"Certainly," says the warden. "Let me know if you need anything."

Hoyle wants to know where I am. They're going to keep a close, close eye on everything I do. I can't ask for the rest of my money from the warden's cage without tripping every alarm in the silent network of watchers cloaking me. A copy of the Hotel Firebird's house rules is taped inside my door, the paper dull yellow and cracking with age. I peel it away, carefully, as it's the closest thing to formal letterhead I'll find here. On the empty, bottom third of the page, I write instructions that the remaining contents of my property envelope, currently secured in the warden's lobby cage, should go to the bearer of this letter, minus any overdue rent, in the event of my absence.

The letter is not legally binding, the warden has no compelling reason to comply instead of keeping it for himself but, if Jack and the Beanstalk can get me out of the Firebird without Hoyle knowing, then at the very least I owe them my good intention and effort. I hand the paper to Jack, then throw a couple of clean shirts, some socks and my toothbrush into a pillowcase. As I do all of this, Beanstalk is busy closing my window and drawing the curtains. He makes a twisting gesture with his wrist at my doorknob. I hand him my key, which he slides into the lock and, with shocking ease, snaps off the end, leaving its teeth lodged in the tumbler. The three of us leave room 621, Beanstalk closing the door as we step out.

"Follow me," says Jack.

We take the stairs to the third floor, to a room at the very end of the hallway near the fire exit. ALARM WILL SOUND, it says.

"There's stairs out there, instead of a fire escape. Much easier and less conspicuous," says Jack. "We need to wait."

"For what?"

"They'll be calling on you in an hour. They won't have an exterminator in tow, if your suspicions are correct."

"I know that."

"They called your room to verify you're there. They'll see from the street that your window is closed, and find your door is locked from the inside." Jack knocks on the door, near the fire exit.

"They're going to think I've locked myself in there. That I've slit my wrists, or something."

"Yes, they will. And as long as they think you're in there bleeding to death, they won't be looking for you at the bus station. But we need to wait until they come knocking."

A woman opens the door, Beanstalk's height but with Jack's shoulders.

"There's my baby," she says. Beanstalk steps into her and they embrace like mother and son reuniting. She whispers into his ear and he strokes her back and arms tenderly. "I thought I heard you out here," she says to Jack.

"Did we wake you?"

"I've had my beauty sleep, Jackie." She takes his hands and bends to give Jack a soft, lingering kiss on the lips. I can see into her room. It's the size of a large closet with barely enough space for her bed, a chair, a piece of wood propped on a pair of milk crates and a mirror leaning against the wall. The floor, bed and wood plank are littered with makeup, lingerie, shoes and broken hamster pipes stained black.

"You brought a friend," she says.

Jack introduces her, "This is, Donna."

"I'm Eric," I say, hoping to avoid any greeting more intimate than giving her my name.

"My pleasure, Eric." She takes my hand, her own larger than Jack's and she smiles with teeth like new porcelain. "You must be 621."

"Eric needs to stay here for a while. No more than an hour," says Jack.

"Were you bad, Eric?" She strokes the back of my knuckles with her free hand.

I want Jack to stay with us, but think better of asking.

"A lot of people seem to think so," I say.

"Of course you can wait here, sugardrop." Donna steps aside and, much to my relief, Jack steps in first.

"Jackie doesn't trust me with you," Donna says.

"If I didn't trust you, I wouldn't have come here," says Jack, taking a seat on the lone chair inside, which leaves the bed to me and Donna.

Donna rolls her eyes. She speaks to me in a stage whisper, "He is so smart. Did you know he's got a doctorate?"

"Donna, please," says Jack.

"And sugardrop here," she juts her massive jaw toward Beanstalk, "he's read every book in the library. Every one. He started at 'A' when he was just a little boy and read all the way to 'Z.'"

"Donna, we need to get him inside. You can work your charms once he's out of sight."

I convince myself I can stand in one place for an hour. I step forward, but Donna blocks my way, standing more than a whole head higher than me.

"Nobody rides for free, sugardrop." She hasn't let go of my hand. She leans into me and I'm too scared to recoil.

"I'm not gay."

"Neither am I, sugardrop."

Her lips envelop mine, soft and pillowy, tasting of cherry lip gloss or bubble gum residue. Her tongue flits once, grazing my upper lip. Her breath is like cinnamon, her hands are like my father's. Her kiss is nothing like yours. I still see your flaming hair that they tell me never existed, and I try to remember what you smell like but it's choked in sweet cherry, cinnamon and bootleg perfume.

"Somebody's in love," Donna says. "It's all over you."

"The worst kind," says Jack.

Donna takes me into her room, closes the door and slides two deadbolts shut, then sits me down on the bed beside her. She wears a purple tube top beneath a pink velour sweat jacket, unzipped to flaunt her chemically enhanced cleavage. Above her sweatpants, a wedge of belly shows muscle that could only have come from doing crunches in her sleep, and her pants themselves are loose enough to camouflage whatever the electrical tape couldn't.

"The worst kind," she repeats, removing her socks. She begins filing her toenails and says, "Jackie means the kind you can't fulfill." She cocks an eyebrow at me. "Am I right?"

"Yeah," I say. "Something like that."

"Your baby in jail? Or did she run away?" She puts the nail file down and takes a bag of cotton balls from her makeshift nightstand, stuffing them between her toes. "Or," she says, "she just somebody you made up?"

"Donna," says Jack. His metronome voice doesn't change, but there's a silent shift in the pitch, some dog vowel that I can't hear but I know is there, and it's as stern as I've ever heard him. "Are we intruding?"

"Not at all, Jackie."

"Because if we're inconveniencing you at all, we can be on our way."

Donna's shaking a bottle of nail polish but puts it aside for the moment to look me in the eye, once more taking my hand into her oversized palm.

"I'm sorry, sugardrop. I didn't mean to pry. I don't get many visitors. At least not the kind who just want to visit. I forget my manners, sometimes."

"Don't worry," I say. "It's no problem."

I've been so distracted by her that I didn't notice Beanstalk isn't with us.

"He's keeping watch," Jack says, before Donna even lets go of my hand.

"Outside?"

"No, he's on the sixth floor. As soon as they come knocking for you, he'll be down. When you don't answer and they can't open the door, that's when they'll assume the worst. The cage man will scramble for his key and when it doesn't work, he'll call for help and all eyes will be on 621. By the time the ambulance, SWAT team, or whoever else has arrived and your door's been kicked open, you'll be gone. I'm assuming you're going to the bus station."

"I suppose. But they'll be looking for me there."

"Not until they realize you're gone."

Donna passes the time painting her toenails and regaling us with stories about shoe shopping and jail. When both of her feet are done she says, "Blow on 'em for me sugardrop, just a little. Don't worry, I'll behave." I cup my palm under her heel, raising her toes slightly, and her foot is the size of a small swim fin. I blow gently, and Donna moans softly. "Shame. All of the good ones are spoken for." She picks up a hamster pipe from her crate-and-plank vanity setup, taking a long, luxurious hit, and the hissing blue flame from her butane lighter sounds like a faraway tornado tearing up the horizon. I think. I'm not sure if I know what that really sounds like. She offers the pipe to me but I decline, then passes it to Jack.

"So tell me what's wrong, sugardrop. Who's after you? What did you do that's so bad?"

I don't want to go into it, not here, not with what could very well be my own product being vaporized in front of me, but something tells me I should at least try for some recognition, throw out a line and see if my delusions run deeper than I already know.

"You ever tried Desiree?" I ask. Saying your name out loud makes my heart beat faster and the metal taste of electricity burn my tongue.

"I told you I don't swing that way," says Donna.

"That's not what he means," says Jack.

I extract one of the blue pills from my jacket pocket, careful not to tip my hand by showing how much I'm holding.

"I mean these," I say. "Desiree, Cradle, Skin." I drop the glossy tablet into Donna's massive palm.

"Oh yes. Yes I have, but I heard they're real scarce, all of a sudden. You holding any more?"

I look to Jack, who shakes his head, no thank you, but I'm not sure what to say to Donna.

"In exchange for my hospitality," she says.

I hand her four more, and she wraps them into a tissue, tucking it down her cleavage.

"Why do you ask?"

"What if I told you I invented it?" There's a pause before Donna starts laughing, a deep, raspy laughter that doesn't match her sugary, bubble-gum girl voice. She gives me a dismissive wave with her painted and glittery fingernails, and fires up the glass pipe once more.

"Somebody had to," Jack says. "And that somebody is local, that much we all know."

"So, you believe me?" I ask.

"Do you?" he asks back. Fair question.

Someone knocks.

"Right on schedule," says Jack.

Donna wants one last grope, but Jack is feeling expedient and steps between us, pushing me out her door as Beanstalk steps inside. Beanstalk remains behind, presumably spooning and sharing the glass pipe with Donna.

"There you are." Jack is standing with me at the end of the hallway, in front of the fire exit. If there's any commotion three floors above, it's not loud enough to hear. "The bus station is close. Halfway to the theater, make a right. You'd be wise to move quickly."

"What about the fire alarm? It'll sound when you open the door."

"Please," says Jack, "a little faith." He pushes open the door to nothing but the sound of the afternoon traffic. "I'm terrible with goodbyes," he says.

"Listen, Jack. Thank you." I'm not sure what to say. "You've done more than—"

Jack closes the door with neither ceremony nor parting sentiment before I'm halfway finished. I stare at the gray metal door, my pillowcase of clothes in hand for a few moments, with no company but the sounds of car horns below and flapping pigeons above. I don't hear any sirens, helicopters, pounding doors or my name being shouted three floors above but somewhere, this very moment, a dispatcher is relaying the warden's frantic call to the authorities, and the authorities are on Hoyle's payroll. I hurry down the stairs and head for the bus station.

The man at the ticket counter is at least eighty years old. He wears a bolo tie with a blue cowboy shirt, and a strip of feathery, ash-colored hair rings his liver spotted head. He can't stop trembling.

"Good evening, sir. Where are you headed?"

They don't know I'm gone. My trial is adjourned and I can still go back tomorrow.

"Littlerock," I say. "Highway 138, toward Nevada. Anything going that direction?"

"Yes sir," he says. "Most folks go *through* there, not *to* there. But you're in luck. We've got one bus leaving shortly."

After I have my ticket, I take my pillowcase to the gift shop inside the bus terminal where I find a cheap, canvas beach bag with "Hollywood" silk screened on the side, and use it to carry my belongings instead. At a liquor store across from the terminal, I pick up bottled water and fruit juice, knowing a long walk in the desert heat is waiting for me. I eat a deli sandwich, chase it with a carton of milk and four painkillers. The fire is returning to my back, so I pick up a quart of whiskey for good measure.

The bus terminal is empty except for me and the ticket vendor. My bus number is nowhere to be seen, and there's no announcement for my platform number or any other.

"Help you, sir?" He wears a military-pressed, navy blue driver's uniform and cap, straight out of a vintage safety film.

"I can't find my platform," I say.

He asks politely to see my ticket.

"That's my bus." He punches my boarding card and makes a note on the envelope. "Your lucky day. You got the whole coach to yourself. Luggage?"

"No. Just my bag."

"Down the ramp, outside to your right. We'll be departing in three minutes."

It's still not too late. I can pay for the lock on my room and check back into the Firebird to finish out my trial. There's a chance, however slim, that I'll be granted a mistrial, or the judge will throw out more evidence. I'm doing nothing but taunting myself with a half day of freedom.

I make my way down the ramp.

A lone bus waits around the corner. It looks as though it had been built fifty years ago but never used, the kind on display at automotive museums or used on movie sets. The brilliant chrome flares in the setting sunlight and, from the open door, I smell brand new leather from the seats, as though the whole vehicle was dropped out of the sky through a hole in time. I have it all to myself. One last look around, but I see nobody watching me, nor anybody trying too hard to look as though they're not. The terminal is empty but for one bus, one driver, and one passenger. I sling my bag over my shoulder and approach the platform. Before I step aboard, I catch the destination placard above the front windshield, giant block capitals, white on black. It reads, PEARBLOSSOM HIGHWAY.

twenty-seven

WHAT I THINK I REMEMBER HAS CHANGED, BUT WHAT I WANT TO REMEMBER has not. The names, numbers, directions, times and formulas, these details slip from beneath my memory like dots of mercury. The movement of one changes the symphony of them all. I remember impressions. I remember sound, color, smells and most of all, touch. I shook Anslinger's hand, but not Morrel's. I shook Jack's hand but never Beanstalk's, though they were always together. I never shook White's hand but his son carried me once, though none of those sensations ever came back to me on my bed at the Firebird. You did, your hands did, every time. I never doubted you were real, and I've never had cause to prove as much to myself or anyone else.

I awaken to a barren stretch of highway in the middle of a barren stretch of nowhere. The view from my window could be familiar if there were anything to remember among the shrubs, cacti and power lines. If anyone boarded the bus while I slept, they left before I woke. We stop where no other bus has in decades, on a dirt turnout marked by a pair of half-submerged tires.

"Have a pleasant evening, sir." The driver tips his cap to me as I depart.

"You do the same."

The door closes and the bus pulls away empty, as clean as it was when I boarded and shining in the setting sun. My back to the highway,

I'm standing at the white tire markers and though I stole a glance at the building behind me as the bus stopped, I'm afraid to turn around just yet. I run my fingers over one of the tires, cracked with age and warm to the touch, and scoop a handful of dirt that I let trickle through my fingers. I remember stopping here before, my red Galaxie shining in the sunlight.

Across the highway, the remains of a concrete dinosaur stand guard in front of an empty swimming pool and condemned hotel, adjacent to an abandoned gas station. I approach the dinosaur and the rebar is still hot from its day in the desert sun. Running my fingers over its chipped, green skin, I feel happy for the first time since I remembered your face.

This is the first time the world outside my head has matched the world inside. I met White four miles from here. This is where I last saw Otto and this is where I last spoke with you.

It's getting dark and the painkillers are fading. My skin cracks when I move. My lips are splitting at the corners and there's not enough water in the oceans to fill me up. My back is bleeding. I have an infection and a fever.

Most every room of the motel is locked and boarded up. The few that aren't stink of mold and stagnant water, their furniture shredded by nesting animals. On the second floor, room 229 has a gap in the plywood where I can reach through and unlock the door. Inside, the room is sparse but prey to nothing worse than dust and neglect. I close the door and prop a chair beneath the knob. Biting into a clean sock, I dump whiskey over my back, then use what little remains in the bottle to chase the last of my painkillers and I pray for sleep.

twenty-eight

EVERY SECOND OF MY LIFE THAT IS WITHOUT WITNESS IS A SECOND THAT never ticked. Every witness to my life prior to my awakening in jail has either been erased by an eight-second black hole or conjured from the smoking remains of my brain, to be dispersed into nothing. Everything prior to this second is a blank that I've filled in with you, and you taught me how to fill in those blanks. I don't know whether I invented the drug that invented you or if I invented you first and the drug came second. I do know that I fell in love with the moment of falling in love and I wanted to keep that moment alive forever, at the expense of all those moments to follow. If I made you from nothing, then maybe I am God, and because I want More, maybe I'm the Devil.

The phone booth looks exactly as it did in my memory, new glass and polished chrome as though it had been built this morning. There's a dial tone and, several quarters later, a ring.

"Anslinger."

"Detective."

He hears my voice then speaks to the room without covering his receiver and says, "He's on the line."

"Thanks," I say.

"For what?"

"Not treating me like an idiot, like I'm crazy. You're supposed to play it casual, act pleasantly surprised while you signal your crew to run a trace, send a tapeworm burrowing into my ear."

"I know you're crazy, Eric. But I also know you're most certainly no idiot."

"But you're tracing the call anyway."

"Yes, I am. You feel like saving me the trouble?"

"Why would I do that?"

"Because you're making it worse," he says. "You skipped out on your trial. The judge made a guilty ruling in absentia."

"If I said where I'm calling from, Detective, you wouldn't believe me."

Muffled voices in the background and a rustle of paper. Anslinger murmurs a thank you to someone on his end.

"I already know," he says.

Time.

"So, you also know you lied to me."

"I never lie."

"You said this phone was out of order."

"I said the line was dead. You weren't exactly at your best when you last tried to dial out of there."

The desert sun burns bright overhead, but the storm clouds are moving in from the distance, a black sheet that will cover Pearblossom Highway come sunset.

"You need to come back, Eric. Or are you going to make me come get you?"

"Yes."

"Why?"

Blood symphonies play in my ears, thoughts form and I dictate the music of my memory, note for note.

"Toe Tag is real."

"It's too late for that, Eric."

"Come get me and you'll see for yourself."

"He's there?"

"Not yet. He'll be coming with his father. I owe them something I can't deliver and they won't risk keeping me around if I'm empty-handed. You're probably the last person I'll ever speak with."

"That's how you want it? How about waiting until we get there?"

"They can't know you're coming. You need to see them."

"I believe you, Eric."

"No, you don't."

"Eric."

"I killed someone," I say. I feel like I've been punched in the neck. The moment I've said the words, I don't care who arrives first, the cops or the Chain. Confessional relief floods from my heart and through my eyes, down my hands and all over the receiver. The last puzzle piece falls into place.

I love you, Dee.

"I wasn't parked here when I started the fire," I say. "White brought me back for my last week at the lab."

"What was your car doing there?"

"I lent it," the punch to my neck again. I press the receiver to my shoulder and breathe, forcing my throat open. "I lent it to someone. She was coming for me."

"Who?"

"I can't say her name."

"Try."

"I can't."

"We searched everything, Eric. There were no traces of anyone else there. Just the dog, Otto."

"And it was hot enough to melt the sand too. Otto belonged to her.

She had my car and she drove out to get us. I heard her outside and thought I was being raided. I lit the fire myself."

"You just confessed, Eric. Not that it matters now, but I'm recording this call."

"I just confessed to a murder."

"Eric, stay there. We're coming for you."

"I'm not going anywhere."

The black sheet is closer, the desert floor below it almost as dark.

"Detective."

"I'm still here, Eric."

"Detective, I'm sorry about what I said. About your daughter."

"I'd forgotten all about it."

"One last thing. You're going to get here and find White and his son. They're dangerous, so bring as many men as you can. White drove me here. He's real. She followed with my car. She was real. You'll believe me when you get here."

"I will. Now, stay where you are, Eric."

"I have to get inside. There's a storm coming. The roads might be flooded, Detective. Tell your men to be careful."

"I appreciate that, Eric."

"Time." I hung up. Old habit.

I dialed information and had the operator connect me with Ford's. Lou answered. No mistaking his voice.

"Manhattan White."

"Who is this?"

"That's not important. I need you to relay a message to Manhattan White."

"I don't know what you're talking about."

"I have Desiree. And his money."

Silence, but for the music in the background.

"I have your attention now," I say.

"I'll pass your message along. Where are you?"

"Tell Manhattan White I'm at the hotel across from the abandoned gas station, down the road from Oz."

"Anything else?"

"Tell him to hurry."

If I choose to believe that Skin was my creation, and is thus proof that I drew breath for a lifetime, then I believe I have swallowed all that was left from the Glass Stripper, which might mean I have swallowed all that was left anywhere. Nothing to do now but to wait for the opposing witnesses to my life, Anslinger and Manhattan White, to arrive and stand witness to one another. If I'm still conscious to face the consequences of my actions, then at the very least I will know that my actions were real, that they indeed had consequences, though my lone life will amount to less than a single click of static in the symphony of the big bang. If my actions were real, then so were my memories, and if those were real, the things I've done have allowed me to see God and I'm not afraid of following my life down that eight-second black rabbit hole.

The approaching swarm of silent helicopters pushes a wall of wind across the desert, blowing great clouds of sand into the air and I hear each grain colliding with the other, culminating in a storm of static as the memories I've conjured forth drag the others with them back to the desert with me. The bleeding shadows from the phone booth and the dinosaur flicker red and blue in the light of the distant lightning. Their shadows jump and I count, *one thousand, two thousand, three thousand,* and onward, but the stormtrooper angels are still some distance away. The red and blue lighting flashes without ceasing, silent but for the coyotes' siren howl carried on the billowing dirt clouds.

I see your face, twisted in pain like I saw it each time I hurt you, but this time it's twisted in the last split moment of pain before your flaming hair erupted for real and your dying breath turned your lungs to plastic.

The smell of rain hits the warm asphalt below, the sound of it pounding in sheets on the roof of the motel like a billion locusts descending at once. They crash onto the gravel rooftop and scurry for a vantage point, searching the cracks for signs of me, and this time, they're not moving on the edge of my vision. They're swarming in plain sight across the parking lot lit by the incessant red and blue lightning, legions of them, taller than me in their black bug armor and telescopic eyes. Peering through a crack in the plywood, I don't see Anslinger or White, yet, but I step away from the window because the bugmen will find me soon enough and I'd rather spend these last minutes with you instead of them.

The last time I heard thunder, it was you hammering on the door of Oz, looking for Otto and me. I thought you were God and I overreacted. I'd been alone and awake for days, and my last human contact had been the cold, quiet drive with Manhattan White, who left me marooned at Oz until I finished the job at hand. If I'd walked to the top of the stairs, opened the front door and stepped into the imaginary storm, I would have instead stepped into your arms with Otto and none of this would have happened. We would have driven away in the Galaxie and you'd still be alive.

This time, it's God, I know because the motel is rumbling like the house did when I was a boy, the windowpanes rattling from the thunder of angels storming the walkways. The red and blue lightning is flashing too rapidly to bother counting, but I try. *One thousand, two thousand, three thousand, four thousand, five thousand,* and a blast of thunder sends a door on the floor below me crashing to the ground. I know that sound all too well. I hear my name amid the cacophony of shouting, then a second door and a third blow from their frames and my room shakes with the fury of these angels. The cellar door held them at bay a long time ago, but the doors of this condemned motel couldn't even to hold back a squatter like me.

Your dry fingers lace with mine, knuckle to knuckle and the waterfall of fire from your hair drapes over my shoulder, spilling down my chest and back as your breath grazes my collarbone and your skin fuses with mine, our beating hearts brushing one another. I hear 223 blown from its hinges by an angel's boot heel and I don't think it could possibly get any louder, but then the thunder sounds again and 225 explodes, and it is louder. They're close, so close the fireflies are swarming through the cracks in the walls and the plywood covering the windows, the little red dots flicker in and out of my line of sight but they haven't seen me yet.

Your breasts are against my back, your lips buried in my neck and your open palms spread across my stomach. You were real, and if I could make you unreal and spare you the pain that I caused you, I would. The angels break down door 227 and I swear they must have kicked it to the back of the room because I hear it hit the bathroom mirror. I'm waiting for the next tell-tale rumble but it's lost in the white noise of the storm and then in an instant the fist of God comes through my room, glass from the bathroom window explodes and a shimmering firefly dances on the wall in front of me, leaving a red needle tracer in the cloud of dust and debris in the air and then the door, my door, with the sound I've been dreading since I woke up so many days ago, flies away and from out of a rushing wall of smoke and rain and noise, burst the black-armored bugmen—angels, call them what you will—dripping wet from the storm clouds they've just dropped through, hurling a swarm of fireflies into my room and this time the swarm converges on me and stays. In my last second, the last of the evidence hits my bloodstream and in the moment before the angels turn off my universe, God's own clock quicksand slows to an ice whisper quiet and I could sit here beside you and watch the sunlight wither for days on end.

acknowledgments

David Poindexter saw to it that I continued to write, above all else. Jason Wood redlined every draft with his merciless eye for detail, as only a good editor and great friend can, and J.P. Moriarty came through when I needed him the most.

I'm forever indebted to Dennis Widmyer and Chuck Palahniuk for breathing new life into my work, which would not have been possible without the sole effort of every author's dream fan, Wendy Dale. I can only hope I'm half the writer, and half the friend, that Will Christopher Baer has been, my brother in all ways but blood.

My friends and family have been a source of constant support on every level, especially Shannon Wright, Charlie Wright, Jim Matison, Scott Krinsky, Damir Zekhster, Todd Bogdan, Paul Fritz, Becky Fritz, Susan Marshall and David Marshall, and my brother, Mick.

I owe my presence behind the Velvet curtains to Kareem Badr, Roland Gaberz, Mirka Hodurova and Kirk Clawes. The good souls at MacAdam/Cage continue to bring my work to light, thanks to the efforts of John Gray, Maureen Klier, Julie Burton, Melissa Little, Avril Sande, Melanie Mitchell, Scott Allen, Jeff Pappas, Jeff Edwards, and especially Dorothy Smith. Thanks to the bookstore crew, Rayshaun Grimes, Kate Schwab, Wayne Jessup, Susan Zussman and Jeff "Big Sexy" Seibel.

Many thanks for many reasons are due to Ray Bussolari, Jim Lambert,

Jeff Aghassi, Heather Fremling Bowser, Caty Farley, Jamie Bishop, Layla Lyne-Winkler, Brad Gustavson, Jacob Berman, Jimmy Kallos, Dawn O'Brien, Brett Redfield, Brian Wagner, Chris Casilli, Scott Fegette, Logan Rapp, Todd Buranen, Staci Buranen, Sarolyn Boyd, Lynda Martin, Jennifer Vaisman, Brenda Mills and the whole Red Room crew.